JASON and the LOSERS

GINA WILLNER-PARDO received a bachelor's degree from Bryn Mawr College and a master's degree from the University of California at Berkeley. She has worked as an editor and now writes full time.

Ms. Willner-Pardo lives in California with her husband and their two children.

JASON and the LOSERS

GINA WILLNER-PARDO

AN AVON CAMELOT BOOK

AVON BOOKS
A division of
The Hearst Corporation
1350 Avenue of the Americas
New York, New York 10019

Copyright © 1995 by Gina Willner-Pardo
Published by arrangement with Clarion Books, an imprint of Houghton Mifflin Company
Visit our website at **http://AvonBooks.com**
Library of Congress Catalog Card Number: 93-44156
ISBN: 0-380-72809-5
RL: 4.5

First Avon Camelot Printing: November 1997

CAMELOT TRADEMARK REG. U.S. PAT. OFF. AND IN OTHER COUNTRIES, MARCA REGISTRADA, HECHO EN U.S.A.

Printed in the U.S.A.

OPM 10 9 8 7 6 5 4 3 2

To Dinah Stevenson, with thanks.

Chapter 1

"Is that enough space?" Everett asked Jason. "Because if it's not, you can have all the drawers. I can keep my stuff in the closet." He opened the closet door too hard and it banged against the wall. "Unless you want the closet," he said.

Jason pulled some T-shirts out of his suitcase and shoved them into an empty drawer.

"I don't care," he said. "I won't be living here for very long. Probably."

Jason didn't know his cousin Everett very well. The only other time they had met was at Great-Aunt Mary Elizabeth's funeral when they were six. All Jason could remember about Everett was that he laughed at all the wrong times, like when Grandma was talking about Great-Aunt Mary Elizabeth's spoonbread and had to blow her nose.

And now Jason had to live with him. And share his drawers.

Everett walked over to the bed. His bare feet made sticky sounds on the floor. "I've never shared my room with anyone before," he said. The bedsprings squeaked as he sat down. "It's going to be fun." When Jason didn't say anything, Everett said, "Don't you think it's going to be fun?"

Everett's jumpy talking was making Jason nervous. "I had my own room at my house. I liked it," he said. "I miss it." He stopped unpacking and looked around. "You've sure got a lot of stuff in here."

Jason had never seen a room like Everett's before. Books and magazines and rocks and leaves and feathers and bottle caps and shells and marbles covered the desk and every bookshelf.

Jason didn't see any trophies. In his room at home, he had fourteen trophies.

Everett blinked and squinted, like someone had shone a flashlight in his face. "Yeah," he said. "I collect things. I have to do my homework sitting in bed."

It was a relief when he stopped talking, Jason realized.

It didn't last very long.

"I can't wait for you to meet my friends. Alvin

and Flea and Frances. Frances is a girl. Alvin lives with his grandparents. You should see his train set."

"A girl? Gross," Jason said. When Everett didn't answer, he asked, "What kind of name is Flea?"

"He loves bugs. Any kind of bugs. He has an ant farm and everything. My mom makes me wash my hair after I go over there, though," Everett said. "Also, his real name is Felix."

He looked nervously at Jason. "I really think you'll like them," he said. He sounded like Jason's mom at parties when she worried that no one was eating any dip.

That was a long time ago. When she had parties.

Jason wished Everett didn't care so much about whether or not Jason liked his friends. "They just sound different from my friends. That's all."

"What do you mean?" Everett unbuttoned his shirt and threw it onto a pile of dirty clothes behind his wastebasket.

"Well." Jason thought. "My friends don't know about stuff like trains and bugs. What they know about is who got traded to the Yankees and how to make a really good corner kick."

Everett nodded. "Like Matt Morrison. He's always captain on teams. It just seems like everybody else has always known how to play everything. I got sick of being the one who didn't know the rules." He sighed. "How did you learn the rules?"

Jason rummaged around in his drawer, feeling for his favorite pjs. "I don't know." He pulled out the pajamas. "I just thought you were born knowing."

"Well, you're not," Everett said.

"I guess," Jason said. He slammed the drawer shut. "At my real school there's this kid. Dexter McGinnis. He played peewee baseball the year we were in first grade."

Everett looked interested.

"Dexter never got a hit. Not one hit. Not even when they gave him a tee to bat off of. And he couldn't remember which was left field and which was right."

Everett nodded.

"Kids were mean. They called him names," Jason said. "Dexter quit after three practices." He stuffed his suitcase under his new bed. "Dexter always got a lot of styes. And he always had a crummy lunch, with things like lemon yogurt for dessert."

Everybody called Dexter a loser. At Jason's school it was the worst thing you could call a person.

Everett went to brush his teeth. When he came back in, he asked, "Are you friends with this guy Dexter?"

4

"He was never on any teams," Jason said, getting up for his turn in the bathroom. "Most of my friends are on teams."

Later, after Everett had turned off the lights, Jason asked, "Don't you guys play any sports at all?"

"My mom is teaching me to play badminton," Everett said.

"I'm not even sure where my mom is," Jason said.

"My mom said somewhere with a beach and no lawyers," Everett said. "We went to the beach last summer. I got stung by a jellyfish and everything."

Jason was barely listening. He lay in the blackness, tears puddling down his cheeks and into his ears. He lay there missing Dexter McGinnis and hoping that Everett couldn't hear him sniffling.

It wasn't even Dexter he missed, he realized. It was his life when Dexter was in it every day. His real life, with his real school and his own room with a closet and drawers both. And his own friends. And a dad who went on business trips and brought him back paperweights and T-shirts with funny sayings. And a mom who didn't even know what badminton was.

"So," Everett whispered in the darkness, "what's it like?"

Jason sniffed and swallowed. "What?"

"Being divorced."

"I'm not divorced," Jason said. "They are." Which was what his mom kept telling him. "My dad has to sell stuff in places like Indiana and Hong Kong. Just like before. I never saw him much anyway."

He didn't tell Everett about how sometimes his dad talked about getting another job and staying put. Jason didn't feel like letting Everett know how much he'd been thinking about that. About living with his dad, instead of with relatives he barely knew.

"My mom has no money," he said instead. "She has to find a place to live since the judge made us sell our house." He swallowed. "She doesn't have much time to be a mom anymore. She has to get a job." He was quiet, thinking. "I don't think she knows how to do anything."

"It's okay, your staying here," Everett said finally. "Except for your stuff all over the place and having no privacy, it's not so bad."

Jason plumped his pillow. "It's just for a while," he said. "Until she gets a job and someplace to live. Then I can go back to my real school. I get to be a crossing guard this year. And there's soccer," he said. "All my friends are trying out for soccer."

"If I went to your school," Everett mumbled sleepily, "I bet I'd be friends with Dexter McGinnis."

Jason felt sick at breakfast. Upstairs, getting dressed, he'd thought about pretending to be sick. Now, sitting across from Uncle Stewart, he thought maybe he wouldn't have to pretend.

"I think I'm going to throw up," he said.

"First-day jitters," said Uncle Stewart, buttering his toast.

Aunt Marjorie set down a bowl of oatmeal. Jason thought that she looked more like a regular mother than his own mom. She wasn't wearing nail polish or high heels. Even though it was getting late, she wasn't telling him to eat faster or looking for clean clothes in the laundry basket and swearing.

"Everett's teacher is a very nice lady," she said. "You'll feel right at home in no time."

"I just started my real school three weeks ago," Jason said. "After summer. Now I have to start all over again."

"It's hard, I know," Aunt Marjorie said. She sounded motherly. Jason's throat closed up. Suddenly he missed his own mom, even though she would have told him to stop whining.

Aunt Marjorie leaned forward and put her hand on Jason's shoulder. "Everything's going to be all right," she said, looking right at him. "Really."

Jason let himself feel okay for a minute. It was nice, not worrying.

"Aunt Marjorie," he asked through a mouthful of oatmeal, "did you ever have a job?"

"Oh, my, yes," Aunt Marjorie said. "For a long time. I was a teacher," she said proudly.

"Oh," Jason said. If Uncle Stewart ever divorced Aunt Marjorie, he thought, she could teach something. She wouldn't have to worry about money. Everett wouldn't have to live with strangers.

"Your mother's very resourceful," Aunt Marjorie said. "She's my sister, after all. I should know."

Jason wondered if Aunt Marjorie had ever lain in bed at night and listened to his mother crying.

"Come on, boys," Uncle Stewart said, reaching for his briefcase. "I'll drive you."

Jason thought it was funny that Uncle Stewart had a briefcase, since Uncle Stewart's job was being Professor Wizard at the University Museum. He wore his regular clothes—scruffy jeans, a T-shirt that said "Kiss a Physicist," and old black basketball high-tops—to work; and his work, Jason thought, sounded very cool. Everett had explained it all this morning while they were brushing their teeth. Uncle Stewart got to do things like use wires to make kids' hair stand

8

on end and give speeches about how the Earth was running out of frogs. Not as cool as being a pilot, Jason thought, but it sounded pretty interesting.

In the car, Everett chattered nervously. "You'll really like Ms. Baker-Huff. Except she's very loud," he said. "Do you like loud teachers, Jason?"

Jason was exasperated. "It doesn't matter. I'm going back to my real school as soon as my mom finds a place to live," he said. "I keep telling you."

He saw Uncle Stewart glance at him in the rearview mirror. He waited, but Uncle Stewart didn't say a word.

So what if I'm rude? Jason thought. He's not my dad. He can't tell me what to do.

On the playground, kids were everywhere. Jason bet there were thousands of them. They were pounding balls against backboards and climbing jungle gyms and playing hopscotch. Some little kids were throwing tanbark at each other. Everyone looked like they already had friends.

Everett was driving Jason crazy.

"Over there's the principal's office. There's a cot for kids to lie down on if they get hit or feel like barfing. The library's down that hall. Our library day is Thursday. Ms. Fisk lets you take out two books at a time, only don't look at her because her eyes look in different places and it's hard to figure out which one is looking at you and which one is looking somewhere else."

The bell rang. "Room Eight. Down this hall," Everett said, sounding important.

Everyone stared at them as they entered Room 8.

One kid whispered, "Hey! Someone's with Stinkball!"

A very tall lady who looked like she had too many teeth in her mouth came over to them. When she smiled, her teeth twinkled. Jason had never seen a grown-up with braces before.

"Jason Gallagher? Everett's cousin? How do you do? I'm Ms. Baker-Huff. That's Baker hyphen Huff. Can you say that?"

Jason was standing right in front of her, but she was yelling as if he were in another room.

"Baker hyphen Huff," he whispered, not thinking.

Ms. Baker-Huff's laugh sounded like a pneumatic drill.

"The hyphen's for spelling, not for saying," she said. "Take that desk by the window, Jason. We start with spelling." She handed him a spelling worksheet.

Jason looked it over quickly. He already knew how to spell everything on it except *ambassador*.

He dug around in his desk and found a pencil, thinking, At my real school, we do reading first.

As he practiced writing *ambassador* over and over, he snuck glances around the room. The kids looked like regular kids. They sucked on their pencils and stared out the window just like the kids at his real school.

Everett's desk was across the room. Everett hunched over it. He bit his lip, concentrating. And just then, Jason saw it happen. It took only a split second, but in Jason's brain it seemed to happen in slow motion, like the replay of a touchdown pass on TV.

Jason saw the kid sitting behind Everett spit a spitball right at him.

It must have stung. Everett's face crunched up and he reached around and rubbed his neck where the spitball must have hit. But he didn't turn around or say a word. The kid behind him made his lips say "Bull's-eye!" and high-fived the kid sitting next to him.

Loser, thought Jason, turning back to his worksheet. A loser named Stinkball.

Chapter 2

"How was it?" Aunt Marjorie asked.

Jason sighed. "Okay," he said.

"I got a hundred on my fractions quiz," Everett said, flopping onto a kitchen chair.

Aunt Marjorie didn't seem to hear. "Did you like Ms. Baker-Huff?" she asked Jason.

"Why does she have to yell everything?" Jason asked.

"Teachers like to be heard," Aunt Marjorie said. She got up to answer the phone. "You'd be amazed how little anyone hears when a teacher talks in a normal tone of voice."

"Still," Jason grumbled. He was hungry and miserable.

"Where were you at recess?" Everett asked. "I was looking for you."

"Around," Jason said. He'd eaten his lunch in the boys' room.

Aunt Marjorie put her hand over the mouthpiece. "For you," she said, and Jason's heart skipped a beat.

"Hi, sweetie," his mom said.

"Hi," Jason said around the lump in his throat. It was hard not to cry when someone you missed called you sweetie.

"How are you, sweetie? How's Everett?"

"Fine," Jason said, because Everett was sitting at the kitchen table listening to everything he said.

"It must be nice to have someone to share a room with," Mom said. "How is school? Do you like your teacher?"

"Not as much as Ms. Jordan," Jason said.

"Well, honey," Mom said, "we just have to make the best of things, I guess."

"What do you mean?" Jason asked. Making the best of things sounded like something you had to do for a long time.

"Just that . . . this isn't easy. For either of us," Mom said. "I miss you."

"So," Jason said, trying to think of something to ask, "what's the beach like?"

"Fine. Lovely," Mom said.

She sounded as though she had never missed anyone in her life. Jason's heart hardened.

"How long do I have to stay here?" he asked.

"Now, Jason. Please. You know I can't answer that. It depends."

"On what?"

"On . . . money and . . . your father and . . ." Mom's voice trailed off.

"I could have stayed with Grant," Jason said stubbornly. "He said so."

"Grant has five brothers," Mom said wearily.

"I know." Sometimes Grant locked himself in the bathroom even if he didn't have to go. Just to be somewhere by himself.

"Everything's so up in the air," Mom said sadly. "Topsy-turvy. I don't know what's coming."

"I have to go, Mom," Jason said.

"Now be good for Aunt Marjorie and Uncle Stewart," Mom said. She sounded perked up. "You'll see, Jason. Everything's going to be all right."

Hanging up, Jason thought that "Everything's going to be all right" sounded better when Aunt Marjorie said it.

"Want to play catch?" he asked Everett, who was pouring himself a glass of milk.

"No, thanks," Everett said.

Jason helped himself to a cookie. "What do you usually do after school?"

"Watch TV. Or work on my stamp collection." Everett took a drink of milk and wiped his upper lip on his sleeve. "Want to see?"

"No!" Without thinking, Jason grabbed another cookie and ran for the back door. He heard Everett yell "Wait" and the screen door slam behind him.

The air was hot and still and smelled like hay. It was the kind of day that made you look for shade and want to move slowly.

Jason ran and ran. His shirt stuck wetly to his back. Sweat streamed down his face.

He wondered what it felt like to have a stroke. He wondered if a ten-year-old had ever had one.

He ran, and his shoes slamming the sidewalk drowned out the hammering of his heart. He gasped for breath, and hot air flooded his throat.

Finally he stopped. He hunched over, his chest almost against his thighs, fighting to fill his lungs. Sweat ran off his face and spattered on the sidewalk.

I could be on a track team, he thought. He and Grant used to argue about which sport was the coolest to do in high school, and Grant always said football because you got to slam into people. Jason always said he didn't think he'd like that part and Grant always said he'd better get used to it or he'd end up doing something like girls' archery.

It was fun, thinking about stuff like that.

Walking back, Jason's head felt clearer. He felt good, all sweaty, as if he could think for the first time since moving in with Everett.

The thing was, he decided, to work really hard

at sports while he had to be away. To run every day, and work on his curve ball, and practice slam dunking. So that when he went back, everyone would make a big deal about how good he was, and how it was really good that he went away and got so awesome.

They would all want him on their teams. He could just see Grant's face.

All that practicing would mean that he would have no time for making friends or getting to know Aunt Marjorie and Uncle Stewart. Which didn't matter, because he was sure that his mom would be sending for him soon. She had sounded lonely, talking about sharing a room and everything.

She'd probably be calling any day now.

Definitely, he thought, opening the back door, no time for looking at a dumb old stamp collection.

Chapter 3

The next day, when the bell rang for recess, Jason ducked into a hallway and followed it to where it spilled out onto the upper field. Kids were kicking balls and chasing each other and yelling things like "Time out" and "Get the girls."

He wanted to kick a ball so badly that he almost felt itchy.

Suddenly he felt a poke. He turned around.

It was the kid who'd shot the spitball at Everett.

"It's Stinkball's friend," said the kid.

"Not friend," Jason said. "His cousin."

A couple of boys standing around laughed.

Jason was curious and scared at the same time.

"Whaddya call him that for, anyway?"

"Because in first grade I threw the ball to him and he threw it back, only he missed and it landed right in a pile of dog doo," said the spitball kid.

Everyone laughed. Jason did, too. He could just see it.

The spitball kid looked at Jason.

"Your cousin's a loser," he said.

Jason looked across the playground. He could see Everett sitting on his bench. Some kids were huddled around. They looked like old men in a park.

"Yeah," he said. He was sure they were going to ask why he wasn't living with his real parents. If they were dead, or if they just didn't want him anymore.

But the spitball kid's reaction surprised Jason.

"Can you play kickball?" the spitball kid asked.

"Yeah," Jason said. He thought about asking what the kid's name was, but he didn't need to.

He was pretty sure the spitball kid was Matt Morrison.

"It's hard to believe that anyone related to Stinkball knows how to play anything," Matt said.

"I'm related to him," Jason said. "But I'm not like him."

"You live with him," Matt sneered.

"Only for a while," Jason said.

"We'll see," Matt said.

They began walking out to an empty diamond on the field.

"You know, you're pretty lucky that I'm even letting you play. Considering you're Stinkball's cousin and everything," Matt said. He looked Jason up and down. "You've got a lot to prove."

He threw the ball to Jason. It bounced, making a sharp, rubbery thump. Jason caught it. It felt pebbly in his hands.

His brain relaxed. His arms and legs were loose and liquid. He felt like his old self.

Jason was up second, after a kid named Chris, who was tagged out. Matt was pitching. He stood stock-still, rolling the ball over and over in his hands, staring right at Jason.

Jason knew a psych-out when he saw one.

He stared right back. He concentrated so hard that he forgot everything except Matt and the ball.

Matt pitched the ball. It rolled straight to Jason, like a bowling ball heading for a strike.

The rubber toe of Jason's sneaker stopped the ball's roll dead and sent it back straight and hard, like a bullet. No bounce. Jason's heart leaped with relief and the pleasure of doing something well.

The ball shot across the infield, passing to Matt's left, just enough to force him to stretch to try and stop it. He missed. Jason, running to first, felt brave and powerful. Weighing his options, and yet somehow without thinking, he rounded first and charged toward second.

The ball didn't waver, didn't bob. Somehow it shot to the right of the outfielder, a kid named Rizzo, who dove for it and missed, cursed, and then looked to see if the yard-duty monitor had heard him.

Jason was at second by the time the center fielder had stopped the ball and thrown it in to Matt.

Jason stood panting, his hands braced just above his knees, his brain too busy to think. It was one of the things he loved most about sports: how there were only the rules, and who was up, and how far you'd run, and maybe, if you let yourself, how it would be if you scored. There wasn't room for more than that in your head. Everything else just got crowded out.

"Whoa, Gallagher!" Matt said. He turned to face home.

Jason took a breath and got ready to run. Matt pitched to another kid, who misjudged the ball and fouled. Everyone yelled things like "sissy" and pretended to walk around like girls.

Just like at my school, Jason thought, inching off second base and leaning toward third.

Kickball was kickball. Rules were rules. If you kicked the ball, you ran. If you missed, people yelled things and made fun of you.

It was nice knowing what to expect.

Matt pitched again and the kid kicked the ball right to him. Matt pivoted smoothly toward third and threw. Running, Jason raced the ball. He wouldn't turn around and go back to second. Turning around would be like admitting he'd made a mistake.

He slid into third. Matt yelled, "He's sliding, you idiot!" and he knew that he'd just beaten the ball. That he'd been fast enough. Barely.

Jason stood up, the length of his left pants leg covered with dust. "Let's go!" he yelled. Third doesn't count, he thought greedily. He wanted to get home.

Then the bell rang. A collective shriek erupted over the playground. Everyone ran for the classrooms.

Rats, Jason thought, pounding his fist on his thigh. Home plate had suddenly evaporated, like a mirage in a desert. He'd forgotten that nothing mattered, that he'd probably be home in a couple of weeks and wouldn't even remember who Matt Morrison was.

He trudged off the field, toward the classrooms.

"How could any relative of Stinkball kick a ball so hard?" he heard Matt ask in a loud voice behind him.

Jason turned around, flattered.

"We're playing the sixth grade next week at lunch recess. One game. Sudden death. The losers have to buy frozen yogurt for the winners," Matt called. "Wanna play?"

"Sure," Jason said. "If I'm still here. Which I probably won't be."

"We have to practice at recess," Matt said, not paying attention. "Every recess. We have to beat them, 'cause I'm no loser!"

Heading toward Room 8, the boys gave each other high fives and aimed pretend rifles at some girls. Chris and Rizzo had a burping contest and argued about who won until Matt said that Rizzo was the loudest. Rizzo looked proud and took several stiff bows.

Jason tagged along, ready in case someone high-fived him, almost hoping that he'd still be around next week, and wondering if anyone else had thought that Chris's burps had been the loudest.

Chapter 4

"Quiet!" Ms. Baker-Huff yelled. She sounded like a drill sergeant. When she turned her back, Matt pretended to look serious, saluted her, and hurried to his seat. Jason turned and smiled, so Matt would know that he'd seen him.

"It's time to talk about your science projects. They're due next week," Ms. Baker-Huff said. "The key to a good science project is asking a good question. Class? What are some good questions?"

Matt raised his hand. "Who is going to win the World Series this year?" he asked.

Most of the boys laughed. The girls looked disgusted.

"Good *science* questions!" Ms. Baker-Huff yelled.

A girl behind Jason raised her hand. "Why is the sky blue?"

"Thank you, Rosemary," Ms. Baker-Huff said. "Let me write that down."

Lots of hands went up.

"How hot is fire?" asked a girl in a blue turtleneck.

"How does a pendulum work?" asked a boy in a backward baseball cap.

"How many stars are there?" asked Rizzo.

After a few more questions, Ms. Baker-Huff turned away from the blackboard. She went to her desk and pointed to a glass jar full of pieces of paper.

"It's pick-a-partner time," she said. "You know the rules. Except for you, Jason. Do you do this at your school?"

"We get to choose by ourselves," Jason said.

"Not here," Ms. Baker-Huff said. "Everybody in the first two rows picks a piece of paper. On each piece is the name of someone from the last two rows. Finders keepers," she said, looking suddenly fierce. "No switcheroos."

Jason unfolded his piece of paper with dread. It said, *Frances Gormley*.

Great, he thought. A girl. Just great.

Everyone was chattering about who they'd gotten stuck with.

Matt came up behind Jason. "Guess who I

got." Without waiting for an answer, he said, "Alvin Jamison. Your loser cousin's friend." Then he socked Jason in the shoulder like it was his fault.

"At least you got a boy," Jason said. He showed Matt his paper.

"Gormley! You got Gormley!" Matt hooted with laughter.

"So?" Jason said. "So what? I probably won't even have to do a science project."

"Everybody has to do a science project."

"Not me," Jason said. Ms. Baker-Huff clapped her hands and all the kids went back to their seats. "Watch this," he whispered, raising his hand.

"Yes, Jason?" Ms. Baker-Huff said.

"Um, I don't think I'll be here long enough to do a project," Jason said.

"Is that so?" Ms. Baker-Huff's voice got quiet. For some reason it was scarier that way.

"Because I won't be here long enough. To finish," Jason said. Everyone was looking at him. His face felt hot.

"But you'll be here long enough to start," Ms. Baker-Huff said quietly.

"Yeah."

Ms. Baker-Huff laughed. "So you'll start, and you'll see what happens. Live in the present, Jason, I always say," she said, sounding like her old, loud self. "No one knows what's around the corner."

Jason slumped in his seat. Ms. Baker-Huff started talking about the Panama Canal, but he barely listened. He drew squiggles in his notebook and wished he hadn't said "Watch this" to Matt Morrison.

But at recess, all Matt said was "It was cool, your trying to get out of doing that dumb old project."

It was funny how Matt saying it was cool made Jason feel cool. Running into home on Rizzo's double, he high-fived Matt without even thinking.

After school, Everett waited for Jason to stuff his books in his backpack.

"I didn't see you all day," he whined. "Not even at lunch. We were waiting for you."

"I didn't want to be late for kickball practice," Jason said.

"We were waiting for you," Everett said again.

Jason zipped his backpack shut. "Just because we're cousins doesn't mean we have to eat lunch together," he said.

He took a step or two back. It always felt like Everett was standing too close, sucking up all the air.

Everett, Jason realized, was standing next to a tall kid with red hair. He was the tallest person Jason had ever seen who wasn't a grown-up.

"I think you're almost as tall as my father," Jason said.

The kid smiled in a funny way and ducked, as if he were used to being punched.

"Flea found a caterpillar," Everett said, "that we wanted to show you."

"Do you like caterpillars?" asked the tall kid with red hair. Jason figured he must be Flea.

"I don't know," he said.

"You're not the kind of kid who likes to step on them for no reason, are you?" Flea asked suspiciously.

"No," Jason said.

"Because I hate kids who go out of their way to step on caterpillars."

"Well, I don't. I just said."

The boys made their way through the halls, which were full of screaming children and grown-ups who looked tired. Jason let himself fall behind Everett and Flea. At his real school he wouldn't have wanted anyone thinking he was friends with kids who waved their arms around so much.

Out on the street, waiting for the light to change, Flea asked, "So what are you going to do for a science project?"

"At my real school," Jason said, "you don't talk about science projects unless it's the day before they're due and you haven't thought of anything yet." He thought. "Or unless you've made something cool, like a bomb."

"I wanted to do something about astronomy. But now Hilary Newhart is my partner." Everett sounded glum. "I bet Hilary hates astronomy."

"I got Genevieve Bruce. She's not so bad. Remember how once her grandparents took her out for dinner and made her try snails? And she liked them! The one I feel sorry for is Alvin," Flea said. "He got Matt Morrison."

"Matt's okay," Jason said protectively.

"He never did get over my throwing that ball in the dog doo," Everett said. "How come he likes you after only one day?"

"I don't know," Jason said.

"I've known him since kindergarten," Everett said resentfully.

"Poor old Alvin," Flea said. "I bet Matt doesn't even know what astronomy is."

"At least he got a boy," Jason said. "I'm stuck with Frances Gormley."

"I wish I'd gotten Frances," Everett said. "She's smart. She works hard. Hilary always says she has a headache and makes you do all the work."

At the next corner Flea waved good-bye. "I have to check on my ants. To see if any of them laid eggs or died or anything," he said.

Sadly, Jason watched Flea head across the

street. An afternoon with just Everett seemed like a long time.

"Don't you guys ever throw a ball around?" he asked.

"Not usually," Everett said. "Actually, never. Come on!" He started running, his book bag banging awkwardly off his leg. "Now I can show you my stamp collection!"

Stamps? "I can't," Jason said.

Everett stopped running.

"Why not?"

"Because after school I do sports," Jason said. "Running and throwing and stuff."

"Why?"

"I don't know. To get better," Jason said. "And because it's fun."

"Aw, jeez," Everett said, turning away and kicking at the sidewalk. "You're just like everybody else."

"So?" Jason asked. "What's wrong with that?"

"Nothing," Everett said. He jammed his hands in his pockets and turned toward home.

Jason headed for the playground. It was almost empty, except for some big kids practicing jump turns on their skateboards.

He took his basketball out of his backpack. He bounced it twice, just for the pleasure of feeling it in his hands, of knowing he could make it do things.

He dribbled the ball the length of the playground and then back again. In the hot sun he began to sweat, but he didn't care. He concentrated on the *thwonk* of the ball as it slammed the pavement, the slap of his sneakers, the in-out rhythm of his breath in his chest.

Next he stood at the foul line, bouncing the ball, turning it over in his hands. He closed his eyes, because sometimes that worked, and pictured the ball sinking neatly through the hoop, swishing through the netting.

On his third try, he scored a basket. And on his sixth. He told himself he wouldn't stop until the ball felt like one of his arms or legs, until his brain just had to tell it where to go and it would go there. By the time the sun was low and not so hot, he almost had it.

Not like everybody else, he thought. Better.

Chapter 5

"How do you like Ms. Baker-Huff so far?" Uncle Stewart asked that night at dinner.

"At my real school Ms. Jordan lets you go to the bathroom if you forget at recess," Jason said. "Ms. Baker-Huff says we're old enough to remember."

"She's a tough cookie," Uncle Stewart said, his mouth full of chili.

"I have to do my science project with a girl," Jason said.

Everett nodded. "He got Frances."

Aunt Marjorie and Uncle Stewart smiled.

It was always that way with grown-ups, Jason thought. They smiled when they were supposed to look sad. They had fun at the beach while you were living with strangers.

They were always doing the opposite of what you expected them to do.

"So what kind of project are you thinking about, Jason?" Uncle Stewart asked.

"I don't know," Jason said glumly.

"I want to do something about astronomy or maybe how maggots live in dead bodies," Everett said.

"If you're interested, I could meet you after school one day at the museum," Uncle Stewart said. "Maybe one of the exhibits will give you an idea."

"Can I come too?" Everett asked, bobbing up and down in his chair. "Hilary and I need an idea too. Can we come? Please?"

Jason thought it must drive Uncle Stewart crazy the way Everett never asked for something just once.

"The more the merrier," Uncle Stewart said. "You boys check with your partners, and we'll set a time in the next few days."

Everett wiped some chili off his chin. Jason thought, I hope no one sees me outside of school with girls.

■

Ms. Baker-Huff made all the partners meet for ten minutes the next morning, after spelling.

Frances was even creepier than regular girls.

"I'm not doing anything about dinosaurs," she said. "I'm sick of dinosaurs."

She scrunched her nose, which, Jason noticed, was covered with freckles. Frances had straight brown hair, brown eyes, and long, skinny arms and legs. Except for the freckles, she looked just like any other girl.

"Do you want to do something about photosynthesis?" Jason asked.

"I did that last year," she sneered.

"How about something with prisms?"

"No."

"Jeez," Jason said. "It's your turn. I can't think of anything else."

"Neither can I."

They sat there. Everyone else in the room was working, making plans. Jason saw Everett. He was talking a mile a minute. Hilary was yawning.

"I don't care what we do," Jason said. "I may not even be here to finish."

"Great," Frances sneered. "Let me do everything."

"Look," he said. He was beginning to feel foolish, just sitting there. "Everett's dad works at the museum. He said he'd show us around and give us ideas."

Frances brightened. "I like Dr. Taylor," she

said. Then her face crumpled back into itself. "I can't go today, though."

Jason looked around. "All the other kids look like they've already gotten ideas."

"Not today!" Frances whispered. "I have ballet."

Jason rolled his eyes. Girls always had ballet.

Frances looked at the floor. "My mom makes me. She says it'll make me graceful."

Who cares? Jason thought. He was never interested in anything girls had to say.

"I don't want to be graceful," Frances said. "I want to be fast."

Actually, Jason wished he were fast, too, but he didn't feel like telling a girl.

"I'm still not doing dinosaurs," Frances said, as if she thought Jason had expected her to change her mind.

"Okay, okay," Jason said. Mainly he wanted to stop talking to Frances Gormley. He knew all he needed to know.

"Let's see what Uncle Stewart says," he said. "Maybe we can go tomorrow."

Chapter 6

"I'm going to ask you some questions," Ms. Baker-Huff said after all the kids had gone back to their seats. "Write your answers down. When we're finished, we'll put all our information into categories. So we'll know more."

Everyone looked confused.

"Don't write your names," Ms. Baker-Huff said. "All information is confidential."

Uh-oh, thought Jason. That's what lawyers said when they asked you questions you didn't want to answer.

"First question," Ms. Baker-Huff said. "What are your parents' first names?"

Jason wrote down *Linda* and *Charles*. It was funny thinking of them that way, without last names. It made them seem like kids.

"What does your dad do for a living?" Ms. Baker-Huff asked.

Jason wrote down *salesman*.

"What does your mom do for a living?"

Jason had to think about that one. Finally he wrote down *nothing yet*.

"Do you live with both of your parents?"

It was the first time anybody had ever asked Jason that. He wrote *no*.

"Do you have brothers and sisters?"

No, Jason wrote.

"What is your favorite color?" asked Ms. Baker-Huff.

Purple.

"What is your favorite fruit?"

Grapes.

"What is your favorite subject in school?"

Jason wondered if kickball was a subject.

"What is your favorite movie?"

Matt raised his hand.

"Can we say 'anything with guts'?"

"No!" boomed Ms. Baker-Huff. "Be specific."

When the bell rang, she collected the papers. "After lunch we'll try to organize this," she said.

Jason felt better knowing that no one else knew what she was talking about either.

He threw away most of his lunch. He only ate the apple and some raisins. He couldn't wait to play kickball, and besides, he wasn't used to sandwiches a mom made. At his real school he had to buy hot lunches in the cafeteria because his mom was always running out of things like mayonnaise.

"Catch!" Matt yelled, throwing him the ball. Jason caught it on the first bounce.

On his first up he kicked a triple. The ball skidded across the grass. Jason tagged the bases, feeling joyous. Out of the corner of his eye he could see the outfielders scrambling.

At third, panting, Jason heard applause. He looked up and saw Everett and Flea standing at the edge of the playground. They were clapping the way you clapped when the principal introduced herself at an assembly.

Jason looked away quickly. He saw Matt on the pitcher's mound. Matt yelled, "Beat it, Stinkball," and looked around. All the other guys laughed and hooted.

Matt looked back at Jason as if he was going to say something, but he didn't. He just looked mean.

Back in Room 8, Jason tried to concentrate. Ms. Baker-Huff had made a lot of columns on the chalkboard, and written things in the columns. Next to each word, she had made different numbers of checkmarks.

"Isn't this interesting?" she said when everybody had quit talking. "Quite a few of you have dads named Dave."

Jason had the only dad named Charles.

"Four Daves," she said. "Out of twenty-four dads." She pointed to the four checkmarks next to *Dave* in the first column. "Who can make this look like a fraction?"

Genevieve Bruce raised her hand. At the board, she wrote $\frac{4}{24}$. "Only it has to be reduced," she said.

"Correct," said Ms. Baker-Huff.

Genevieve twisted her lower lip around with her teeth. Finally she wrote $\frac{1}{6}$.

"One sixth of our dads are named Dave," Ms. Baker-Huff said. "How else can we say this?"

Jason knew she meant percentages. He already knew how to do them from his real school. He worked fast.

"Sixteen and two thirds percent," he called, forgetting to raise his hand.

"That's quite a big percentage," Ms. Baker-Huff said, "when you think of all the names there are."

Jason didn't pay much attention to how many moms were named Barbara and what jobs everybody's parents had. He was more interested in the next column.

Ten kids didn't live with both of their parents. Ten whole kids.

Jason figured it out: 42%, if you rounded up. That was almost half.

Jason looked around. He wondered who else

was in that 42%. Alvin, he knew. That left eight kids.

If something crummy had to happen to you, like your parents getting a divorce, Jason thought, it was nice knowing you were part of 42%. It was nice knowing you weren't alone.

"Before we organized our information," Ms. Baker-Huff was saying, "we had twenty-four papers, each with nine pieces of information. That's two hundred sixteen pieces of information. That's a lot. Too much."

Jason smiled. It was the first time a teacher had ever told him you could know too much stuff.

"By organizing what we know, we can make it more useful," Ms. Baker-Huff said. "We can use information to make decisions. To take action. To see how things are alike and how they are different. To understand how things really are."

Jason wasn't sure knowing how many kids liked purple was going to help him make any decisions.

At lunch, Matt stuck two pretzel sticks up his nose. He tilted his head back to balance them on his upper lip. "Three guesses whose loser father is a wizard," he said.

Jason remembered last night. Uncle Stewart had sat on his bed and told ghost stories that were scary in a fun kind of way, and when he was finished, he'd leaned over and ruffled Jason's hair and said, "Night, big guy." Jason had been afraid that Uncle Stewart was going to kiss his forehead, the way he always did with Everett, but he didn't, and Jason relaxed. It was nice being called big guy. His own dad called him monster man.

If it weren't for Uncle Stewart letting him live there, Jason would have had to live with Aunt Marion, who had bad breath and moles.

"Leave it to Stinkball," Matt was saying. "My dad is an accountant. He has a normal job."

"Let's play," Jason said.

"In a second." Matt was trying to jam pretzel sticks into his ears. "So what's your father, Gallagher? An Indian chief? A ballerina?" He took the pretzels out of his ears and ate them.

"He sells stuff," Jason said proudly. "Cool stuff."

"Like what?"

"Rockets." It was a lie, but it was all Jason could think of.

Jason's dad was always selling something. That part was true. He used to sell little metal things that went into lawn mowers, and steel springs that came in different sizes. Everything he sold was supposed to be a piece that went with something else. Nothing by itself was very interesting.

Jason's dad always said how pieces were important. If a jet airplane was missing a piece, he said, it could crash or explode in midair.

Once in a while, though, Jason wished that his dad would sell the whole jet airplane.

Matt stretched. "So are we just going to sit here, or what?" he asked.

As if Jason had been the one asking all the questions.

Later, waiting for his turn to kick, Jason felt eyes boring into the back of his neck. He turned around. Matt was sitting in the bleachers, his arms crossed across his chest.

Matt cocked his head. "What kind of rockets?" he asked.

Jason opened his mouth, but no words came out. His brain began to sizzle.

"Gallagher! You're up!" Rizzo called from first.

Turning away, Jason felt himself breathe. He felt as if he'd slid into third, just beating the ball.

Fast enough. But just barely.

Chapter 7

After school, Jason found Matt out in the hall-way.

"Sometimes I shoot baskets after school," he said.

"So?" Matt asked.

"So you can come," Jason said. "If you want."

Matt seemed to think about it for a long time. Finally he shrugged. "Anything's better than homework," he said.

Jason's heart quickened. He'd been getting sick of shooting baskets by himself.

They played basketball for an hour.

"Whoa, Gallagher!" Matt said as Jason sank a three-pointer. Jason felt himself flush with pleasure. He retrieved the ball and sat on it, breathing hard.

Matt wiped his arm across his forehead.

"I don't know about you, Gallagher," he said.

"What do you mean, you don't know about me?" Jason said. "What don't you know?"

"What kind of kid you are," Matt said.

He picked up a stick and threw it.

"What's that supposed to mean?"

"Whether you have loser blood in you," Matt said. "You're Stinkball's cousin. You must be at least a little bit like him."

"I'm not," Jason said. "I'm nothing like him." He hunted for a stick bigger than Matt's. "I didn't even know him until a couple of days ago. I'm not like him at all."

Matt smiled a slow smile. "Prove it," he said.

Jason didn't like being told what to do. But having somebody to shoot baskets with had been fun. He didn't want to go back to doing it alone.

"You have to be really mean to him," Matt said. "That'll prove you're not a loser." He wasn't smiling. "Really mean," he said.

"How mean?" Jason asked. "I'm not killing him or anything," he added.

"Really mean," Matt said again.

Sometimes, when Jason's dad was sick of selling things, he talked about what he'd always wanted to do, which was be a forest ranger.

"How'd you like that, huh, Jason?" he'd ask. "Me and you living in the forest with the bears and the squirrels?"

Bears and squirrels weren't so bad, Jason would think. If you were a forest ranger, at least you got to stay in one place. The forest wasn't going anywhere.

Now he felt a flash of anger at his father. If it weren't for his father always running around selling stuff, he wouldn't be in this mess. He would have had a real dad to live with, instead of relatives he barely knew who made him go to a school where he didn't have any friends.

"I don't have to prove anything," he said. "I don't even really live here."

Matt shrugged. Not as if he agreed, but as if Jason weren't important enough to argue with.

"I was in a club at my real school. With some guys," Jason said to Matt. He couldn't stand being unimportant to somebody who always won everything. "We built a fort in the backyard and camped out in it. We ate marshmallows and held flashlights under our faces so we looked like monsters."

It was hard to believe that he'd gone out for pizza with Grant and DJ just last week. They had pulled cheese off their pizza slices and pretended it was stuff coming out of their noses.

"We had an initiation and everything," Jason said. "People who wanted to join had to be blindfolded and put their hands in a bowl of oatmeal." He smiled, remembering. "After we told them it was throw-up."

"Cool," Matt said.

"That was the meanest thing I ever did," Jason said.

He already knew what Matt was going to say next.

Matt said, "That's not mean enough."

Chapter 8

After lunch on Thursday, Ms. Baker-Huff put on her sunglasses and a pair of bright-red sneakers.

"Thursday is P.E. day," she said to Jason.

"Oh boy," Jason said.

Everett's friend Alvin raised his hand. He was short and round, with skin so white it looked almost blue, and huge feet that seemed to have been meant for someone else's body.

"I don't feel well," he said. "And my grandma doesn't like me going outside without sun-screen."

Matt and the guys cackled. Some of the girls rolled their eyes.

"A little sunshine never hurt anyone," Ms. Baker-Huff said. "Everyone will participate today," she said firmly to Alvin.

Ms. Baker-Huff led the kids from Room 8 across

the patio to the playground. A tall, thin man with no hair and a whistle was waiting for them.

"Mr. Perkillo does five hundred push-ups every morning and eats raw eggs for breakfast," Everett whispered to Jason. "You should see his stomach muscles."

Even without turning around, Jason could feel Matt behind him, staring right through him.

"Jeez, Everett," Jason said in a loud voice, "you smell."

Everett's eyes widened and blinked.

Behind him, Jason heard snickering.

Everett jammed his fists into the pockets of his windbreaker.

"Sorry," he said.

Jason looked into the sun and squinted. When he opened his eyes, Everett had disappeared into the crowd of kids behind him.

Jason felt a hand on his shoulder.

"Not mean enough," Matt whispered.

Mr. Perkillo blew his whistle. "Fifty jumping jacks, twenty push-ups, three times around the track," he said.

"How come P.E. teachers never have to do any P.E.?" Jason whispered in between push-up number twelve and push-up number thirteen.

Mr. Perkillo was sitting on the bleachers, fiddling with his whistle.

"P.E. teachers are weaklings," Matt panted. "Even Ms. Baker-Huff can do push-ups."

Jason glanced over his shoulder at Ms. Baker-Huff. He'd never seen a teacher so close to the ground before.

The boys got to their feet and broke into a slow jog down the track.

"I hate weaklings," Matt said. "My dad says never be a weakling because no one will like you and also because weaklings are losers."

They finished their first lap just as Everett hauled himself off the blacktop, gasping and panting, his push-ups finally over.

"My dad says until you're a winner, you're a loser," Matt said.

The boys jogged on. Jason felt drops of sweat snaking down the back of his neck. He could see everyone spread out around the track. He spotted Ms. Baker-Huff walking fast, her arms bent sharply at the elbows, her front shifting from side to side.

He and Matt kept passing everyone. The other guys would sprint a few steps, trying to catch up, only to drop back, pretending not to be breathing hard.

Only Frances ran faster. She passed them, looking straight ahead.

"How come she's so fast?" Jason asked, but Matt just scowled at the cloud of dust that rose behind her.

They jogged past Everett hobbling along the

straightaway. Jason could see his face, bright red and slippery with sweat. As they ran past, Everett looked up and smiled. He raised one hand in a feeble wave.

Jeez, thought Jason. Guys don't wave. Doesn't he know that?

He felt a hand on his shoulder.

"Jason? Jason?" Matt asked, making his voice high and girly. He was waving furiously.

"Shut up," Jason said, but Matt just laughed.

Jason slowed his pace. He could hear Everett behind him, half walking, half jogging, grunting with the effort to breathe.

Jason slowed down until he knew Everett was directly behind him, coughing on the clouds of dust his sneakers raised. He imagined he could feel Everett's breath hot on his neck.

His brain was blank and empty, but somehow he knew exactly what was going to happen next.

"Wait up," Everett wheezed.

Jason veered slightly to his right, braked to a dead stop, and turned, leaving his left foot directly in Everett's path.

Just as Jason had planned, Everett tripped. He seemed to sail in slow motion, oddly graceful, until he thumped heavily onto the dusty track. Jason heard him wail.

All the kids jogged over to stand around and look. Everett lay sprawled facedown across the

49

track, crying. His face was caked with dust and sweat.

Ms. Baker-Huff broke up the crowd. "Now, now, Everett," she bellowed. "We all take a spill now and then. Come on," she said. She hooked her hands under his arms and hauled him to his feet. "Stumbled over your own two feet again?"

Everett shook and sniffled. "Jason's foot," he managed to say.

Ms. Baker-Huff looked at Jason.

"You said wait up," Jason said sullenly.

Everett rubbed his eyes and hiccupped.

"No harm done," Ms. Baker-Huff said. "Have a seat, Everett. Catch your breath."

Everett hobbled to the bleachers. He sat down next to Mr. Perkillo, who was staring vacantly at a nest of squirrels and seemed to have missed everything.

On the track, Matt jogged past Jason. "Nice work," he said, clapping him on the back.

Jason slowed up and let Matt run on ahead. He tried to think of stuff to keep his mind busy, off the dust and how sweaty he was and Everett hunched over and breathless on the bleachers and how hot it was for fall.

With surprise he realized that Halloween was only a few weeks away. Last year he'd been a pirate.

He wasn't in the mood for Halloween. It was

too warm, for one thing. And he couldn't think of anything to be. He was having enough trouble just being himself. He felt like this year, in a costume, the real him might get lost or just disappear.

He finished his laps, hearing only the dust-muffled thud of his sneakers against the track and the hiss of his breath as he exhaled into the hot, still afternoon air.

Rounding the last curve, he glanced up at the bleachers.

Everett looked away.

Chapter 9

After school Everett hobbled over to Jason's desk. He stood waiting while Jason collected his things.

"What?" Jason asked meanly.

Then he remembered about going to the University Museum.

Everett was clenching and unclenching his fists. When his words finally came out, Jason jumped.

"It's *my* room," he hissed. "And they're *my* parents. They're just your *relatives*."

Before Jason could think of anything to say, Everett turned and stormed out of the classroom.

Hilary and Frances were waiting out by the curb. Hilary was putting on nail polish.

"I saw you do it," Frances whispered to Jason. "You did it on purpose."

"Shut up, Frances," Jason whispered back. "He said wait up."

"'Wait up,'" Frances said. "Sure."

Jason wished Uncle Stewart's car weren't so beat-up looking. For Uncle Stewart's sake. "My dad has a sports car," Hilary said. "With a phone."

Nobody talked much in the car. Everett sat in the front, fiddling with the radio. Frances scrunched up as close to the window as she could so she wouldn't bump into Jason. On his other side, Hilary blew on her nails and waved her hands around. "So they'll dry," she explained.

Frances held her nose. "Your hands stink," she said. "They smell like the stuff my dad sprays on the grass to kill weeds."

Jason tried to breathe through his mouth. He hoped he wouldn't get carsick.

The University Museum sat on a hill overlooking the town.

"It looks like a flying saucer that just landed," Jason said.

"There are computers and a snack bar with tuna melts and a real iguana that you can touch and an X ray of a mouse inside a snake," Everett said, turning to look at Hilary. "Wait'll you see."

Hilary looked out the window and rolled her eyes.

Uncle Stewart parked the car and hurried everyone in. "I love to show off the museum," he said. Everett smiled up at him.

For a second Jason imagined hiking in the woods with Grant and DJ and maybe even Matt and Chris. And his dad, in a uniform, telling everyone the names of all the trees and to please stay on the trail.

Uncle Stewart showed the receptionist at the front desk a card from his wallet. "Thanks, Professor Wizard," she said, winking at the kids.

First they went to look at the apatosaurus. It was just a model of one, but you could tell that a lot of little kids weren't sure. Its eyes moved and every fourteen seconds it opened its mouth and roared. Jason knew it was every fourteen seconds because he counted the time between roars.

"How do they know it sounded like that?" he asked.

"Scientists find the bones and reconstruct the skeleton," Uncle Stewart said. "Then they figure out what the muscles must have looked like, and where the organs were. From there, they can deduce things like what the voices sounded like." He smiled. "Science is all about analyzing what you know and making the right decisions."

"Can science answer every question?" Jason asked, but Uncle Stewart was pointing to the elevator.

"The animals are downstairs," he said.

"They have newts," Everett said to Hilary. "I'll show you."

Frances and Jason followed Uncle Stewart into the next room. On the wall were pictures of famous scientists.

Jason stopped in front of Isaac Newton. "'To every action there is always opposed an equal reaction: or, the mutual actions of two bodies upon each other are always equal, and directed to contrary parts,'" he read. "What does that mean?"

Uncle Stewart said, "That's a very interesting principle. It's what makes a rocket fly." He pushed his glasses up the bridge of his nose. Jason knew he was getting ready to explain something complicated.

"Hot, burning gas molecules push against the inside of the rocket. That's the action.

"When these molecules strike the rocket, they bounce backward. That's the reaction.

"Their energy has been transferred to the rocket and causes it to move forward. As the molecules push against the rocket, the rocket pushes back with an equal and opposite amount of force."

"What are we supposed to do?" Frances said. "Launch a shuttle in Room Eight?"

Jason thought for a minute. "Every action?"

Uncle Stewart nodded. "Every one."

"Even something like throwing a ball?"

"Sure," said Uncle Stewart. "The trick is to design an experiment that shows the reaction created when a ball is thrown."

"How do we do that?" Frances asked.

"Think about it for a while," Uncle Stewart said.

On the way downstairs, Jason said to Frances, "If it's all the same to you, I'd like to do something about action and reaction."

Frances looked bored.

"We could do something with balls," Jason explained. "I'm a pretty good ball player."

Frances didn't say anything.

"I don't see you thinking up any great ideas," Jason said.

"It just so happens," Frances said, "that I can play ball just as well as you. Better, maybe."

She marched on ahead.

Just what you'd expect from a girl, Jason thought, following her into the animal laboratory. Making stuff up when she doesn't get her way.

Everett and Hilary were watching newts in a terrarium.

"They're just lying around," Hilary complained.

"They're very interesting," Everett said, "if you just give them a chance."

Hilary examined her nails. "I'm not doing newts," she said. "I want to do snakes!" She looked at Everett. "Snakes are more exciting than dumb old newts."

Jason wandered around the laboratory. There were turtles and mice and an iguana named Beatrice who looked a little like Aunt Marion.

He stopped in front of a terrarium full of frogs. He peered in at them. The terrarium looked cool and secret and full of shadows. The frogs were hard to see. They blended in with leaves and tree bark and were almost invisible unless you looked hard.

Some things about being a frog might not be so bad, Jason thought.

He wondered which were the frogs that hopped funny, or didn't like to eat flies.

He leaned in close to watch. Did frogs have friends? he wondered. Could a frog tell if other frogs didn't like it? Did frogs ever get divorced?

Jason's daydreams evaporated as a shattering scream pierced the animal laboratory.

"Frogs!" Hilary shrieked. "Loose frogs!"

Some seconds passed before Jason realized what had happened. He had edged the metal screen off the top of the terrarium. Frogs had begun to hop out through the gap between the edge of the screen and the top of the tank. There were frogs everywhere, chirping merrily in celebration of their unexpected freedom.

Jason stared at the terrarium in silent horror.

He heard faintly in the background Hilary screaming and other kids whooping in mock terror. Mostly he heard the blood thudding in his head, keeping time with the hammering of his heart.

"Jason!" Hilary was screaming. "Get them, you idiot!"

Jason felt his face burn. A frog hopped onto his shoe, then off again. He knew he should reach down and try to catch it, to cup his hands over it the way he did with Grant and DJ, down by the creek in the summer. But he couldn't move.

The only time other kids had ever yelled at him was when he'd rounded the bases or caught a fly ball.

"Whoa! Frog attack!" Uncle Stewart had opened the door to the laboratory and was loping over to the terrarium.

Even in his misery Jason noticed that Uncle Stewart ran like someone who only ran in emergencies.

Uncle Stewart bent down, collecting frogs. "Help me out, Jason," he said, scooping up two at once. "Everyone else, stand back! We don't want any squished frogs!"

All the kids giggled. Uncle Stewart sounded calm. Even the frogs seemed to relax.

"Jason and I will take care of everything,"

Uncle Stewart said. He looked at Jason and smiled.

Able to move at last, Jason lunged for a frog sitting motionless under a lab table. He was glad to have been assigned a role of importance. It made him feel less foolish.

Standing up, the frog pulsing in his cupped hands, Jason looked straight at Hilary. The look on her face, as if she had just smelled something bad, was new to him.

"What a loser," she said under her breath.

Jason pretended not to have heard her, but his face felt hot again. He looked quickly away, and saw Everett.

Everett looked from Hilary to Jason. His face was frozen, stony. And then, so slowly that it seemed not to be happening at all, his mouth curved into a small smile. He raised his hand waist high and waved.

Chapter 10

That night, looking for his math book, Jason poked his head into the den. Everett was sprawled across the sofa, his eyes glued to the TV.

Jason started to back out of the room.

"It's *Aliens Invade Wisconsin*," Everett said. "You can watch. I don't care."

Jason shrugged. *Aliens Invade Wisconsin* sounded better than fractions.

"This is where they suck out the guy's guts while he's screaming," Everett said, stuffing popcorn into his mouth.

They watched.

"Cool," Jason said.

During the commercial, Jason said, "Have you seen *Space Killers from Neptune*?"

"No."

"It's got a spaceship with lasers and a monster made of slime," Jason said. "You should rent it."

On TV, some fake-looking family was talking about what cereal they ate for breakfast.

"We don't have a VCR," Everett said. "My dad says it would be hard to pay attention to a movie in his own den."

"Oh, yeah. I keep forgetting," Jason said. "What's at my real house, and what's here."

Like which walls the light switches were on. And where the extra toilet paper was. And whether he had to finish vegetables to get dessert.

On TV, the aliens were back. They were chasing some people through an alley. One of them looked like a giant frog.

"Uncle Stewart said they found all of them except six," Jason said. "I don't think six lost frogs is such a big deal."

Everett barely nodded. It was weird, Jason thought, Everett being in the same room with him and not talking.

During the next commercial, Jason took a deep breath. "I know they're just my relatives. I *know* that." He tossed a kernel of popcorn high in the air and caught it on his tongue. "I have my own parents. Even if I don't live with them."

Everett munched for a while. Jason thought he wasn't going to say anything.

But finally he swallowed. "It's just . . ." he started, then stopped, then started again. "Your clothes are in my drawers. Your toothpaste is all over my sink. You don't like stamps or bugs or trains. My mom and dad are always wondering how your day was or what you want in your lunch. And at school you're just like everybody else." He stopped, breathless. "You're hard to like," he said.

"Really?" Jason said.

"Well . . ." Everett hesitated, then looked bravely at Jason. "Yeah."

Jason didn't know what to say. It was funny, how he felt. Not mad at all. Relieved.

"So are you," he finally said.

Everett looked back at the TV. "My mom says be nice to you no matter what," he said. "Because of . . . everything." His voice got quiet. "But it's hard," he said.

Jason didn't like the idea of someone being nice to him because his mom was making him. But telling Everett to stop being nice seemed stupid.

The fake family eating cereal was back. The fake son looked into his bowl, made a face, and sat back in his chair, scowling. The fake dad pounded his fist on the table and said cheerfully,

"Stanley won't eat soggy cereal. It's time to take action!"

Right, thought Jason. A real dad would either figure out how much money you were wasting or hit you.

"Frances and I are doing action and reaction," he said. "We have to figure out how to show the reaction from throwing a ball."

He shoveled a fistful of popcorn into his mouth.

It was weird, Everett not answering him.

"So can Frances really play baseball?" he asked.

Everett nodded, not taking his eyes off the TV. "You should see her. Matt hates her because she got three hits off him in P.E. and all the kids booed and Chris Doniger told Matt to stop pitching like a sissy." He paused to watch some aliens eat a car. "You should see her," he said.

"Wow," Jason said.

They sat in silence for a while.

"Your feet have to be off the ground," Everett said.

"What?"

"Otherwise, you can't see the reaction."

"I don't get it," Jason said.

Everett said, "If you're standing on the Earth, then it's like you're connected to it. Right?"

"Yeah," Jason said doubtfully.

"Throwing the ball—the action—is supposed to move you backward. Only it can't move you and the whole Earth, which is what you're connected to."

Wisconsin was in ruins. The aliens were heading to Minnesota. Not even the good guys could stop them. They huddled in doorways, sponging slime off themselves, trying to stay out of the way.

"Hey!" Jason said. "I think I see."

He looked over at Everett, who was picking popcorn out of his teeth. He hadn't said one word, Jason realized, about Hilary calling him a loser.

"In P.E. today," he said, "I didn't say you had a *bad* smell."

Everett's eyes were glued to the TV.

"I'm always getting tripped. Ever since kindergarten, people have been tripping me," he said. "I'm sick of it."

That night, even though he was sleepy, Jason lay awake in the dark a long time. He listened to the sounds the house made in the night: Everett snoring; the flick and rumble of the furnace going on and off; a spoon clattering against a dish down in the faraway kitchen. It seemed, as he listened, that even the darkness itself made noise. If he listened really hard, he could just make it out, hushed and whispery.

Fading finally into sleep, Jason listened to the whispery darkness and wondered what the darkness at home—the house he used to live in—had sounded like. He couldn't remember.

Chapter 11

"Everett explained it to me," Jason said to Frances at recess on Friday.

He could see Matt and Chris and the others across the playground. They were staring at him.

"What?"

"About why you can't see the reaction when you throw a ball."

Frances looked interested.

"If you threw a ball and you were hanging in midair, you'd go backward, and that would be the reaction," Jason said. "But because you're standing on the ground, you don't move. There's no reaction."

Frances sat down in a swing. "There has to be a reaction," she said. "Dr. Taylor said there has to be."

"Well, there is a reaction," Jason said, "but you can't see it."

Frances dug her feet into the sand. "I guess I see," she said. "But that's not a very interesting science project. We can't just throw a ball and say there's a reaction, but sorry, it's invisible."

Jason snuck a glance at Matt. He and Chris were making big, smacky kisses at him and Frances.

"Don't you have somewhere to go?" Frances asked, seeing Jason looking. "Don't you have to go kick a ball or something?"

"In a minute," Jason said. "If only we could hang in midair, like a tetherball, or a spider from a web."

"Hey!" Frances shoved her feet in the sand and pushed. "Like a kid in a swing!"

Jason laughed.

"Wait here!"

He ran across the playground to where Matt and Chris were picking teams.

"Can I borrow the ball?" he asked. "Just for a second."

Matt and Chris didn't look too friendly. "Are you going to give it to your girlfriend?" Matt asked.

"Shut up," Jason said.

"Ooooh!" Matt said. "He wants his girlfriend to be a secret."

"If I had a girlfriend, which I never would," Jason said, "she would have gotten three hits off you *and* struck you out."

That shut him up.

"Bring it back by the time we're done picking teams," Chris said.

Jason ran back to the swings. Frances was digging a hole in the sand with her toe.

"Here," Jason said. "Now pick your feet up."

Frances bent her knees so that her legs folded up under the saddle of the swing.

Jason handed her the ball.

"Now throw," he said.

She did. And swung backward. Not very far. But enough to see.

Jason and Frances laughed at the same time.

"Now the only problem," she said, "is how do we get a swing into Room Eight?"

The guys looked like they were ready to play.

"I think they need this," Jason said.

Suddenly he noticed some girls from Room 8 hanging on the monkey bars. They were laughing and whispering. Girls were always laughing and whispering, it seemed to Jason.

"Don't you ever play with girls?" he asked Frances.

Frances looked ferocious. "They play hair-dresser and have rules about who you can be friends with." She kicked at the sand with the tip of her shoe. "I don't like rules like that."

"Girls sound a lot like boys," Jason said. "Except for the hairdresser part."

"I like Everett and those guys," Frances said. "Even if they can't throw a ball to save their lives."

"But don't you miss playing ball at school? I mean how do you stand not playing?"

Frances leaned backward in the swing until her head was almost resting in the sand. "My dad plays catch with me every Saturday," she said.

"Hey, Gallagher!" Matt yelled. Jason turned and ran, glad to get away.

"We play the sixth grade in one week," Matt said grumpily. "One week. We don't have time to waste talking to girls."

Jason could see Frances sitting in the swing. She looked like she was digging a hole to China with her shoe.

"Get it, Gallagher?" Matt was saying.

"Okay, okay," Jason said.

She probably didn't mean it to sound like bragging when she talked about playing catch with her dad.

It seemed like a waste of a perfectly good kid, her just sitting there.

After school Jason was heading home when he heard Everett and Frances and the others behind him. "I thought you always played on the playground after school," Everett said.

"Not played," Jason said. "Practiced." He looked

up and down the street. Matt was nowhere to be seen. "I left my ball at home."

"We're going to my house," Frances said. "You can come if you want."

Before Jason could answer, Everett said, "He's busy," in such a loud voice that everyone turned to look at him.

"Yeah," Jason said. "I have to get my ball."

Actually he'd been thinking about going home and doing some homework. He was sick of practicing.

Now he kept a little ahead of the others, unsure whether he was welcome to walk along, or whether he wanted to.

"I can't get Matt to call me back," Alvin was saying. "We decided to grow a plant upside down, only Matt said he's allergic to dirt, so I have to do most of the work."

Jason couldn't help turning around. "Allergic to dirt?"

"I have a cousin who's allergic to milk," Alvin said. "If you can be allergic to milk, I guess you can be allergic to dirt."

Jason pictured Matt sliding into home plate, covered with clouds of infield dust. He started to say something but changed his mind.

"I've got some eggs at home in my ant farm," Flea said. "Genevieve Bruce said it's okay with her to hatch ant larvae for our project. Only she doesn't want to touch any ants. She says ants are creepy."

"Hey, look at that!" Everett was pointing to a house on the corner. It was old and crummy looking. A lot of dump trucks were parked on dirt where a lawn used to be. Some workers were tearing down a fence.

"Who lives there?" Frances asked.

"Some old man," Flea said. "He always gives raisins for Halloween."

"Look at all that wood," Everett said. "I wonder what they're going to do with all that wood."

"My mom could use it," Flea said. "She's building a sandbox for my sisters."

Jason had an idea. "Hey!" he said, looking at Frances, but she'd already thought of the same thing.

The worker tearing down the fence didn't mind. "Be my guest," he said. "Otherwise I just have to haul it away."

Jason forgot about going home. He tagged along to Frances's house, to the toolshed where Frances said her mom kept the wheelbarrows. There were two of them, old and rusty, covered with cobwebs and full of bags of potting soil.

"I bet you can get what you need in two or three trips," Everett said. He climbed into one of the wheelbarrows. "Someone push me."

Jason grabbed the handles and gave Everett a

jerky ride around Frances's backyard. Frances tried to push Flea and Alvin in the other wheelbarrow, but they were too heavy together, so she made Flea get out.

"Let's race back," Jason said, navigating Everett out to the sidewalk and pointing the wheelbarrow in the direction of the torn-down fence.

Alvin, jouncing along, clung to the sides of Frances's wheelbarrow. "Is there such a thing as getting wheelbarrow-sick?" he asked. "Not too fast, Frances!"

Frances didn't answer. Her eyes glittered. She took her position on the sidewalk next to Jason and Everett.

"On your mark, get set, go!" yelled Flea, and they were off, clattering down the sidewalk.

Jason and Frances ran neck and neck, jockeying for position on the narrow sidewalk. Jason thought that he had never seen a girl run so fast. Especially a girl pushing a wheelbarrow with a kid in it.

Alvin, his eyes shut, hung on to Frances's wheelbarrow for dear life. He looked too scared to scream.

Everett, Jason realized in amazement, was laughing.

The race was so close that no one could decide who'd won.

"We beat you!" Frances said, stopping just short of the curb.

"Did not," Jason said, just for the fun of saying it. He didn't really care. He leaned over and high-fived Everett, who high-fived back in a way that made Jason think he'd never done it before.

"It's fun racing," Everett said, "when you don't have to breathe hard."

Jason was laughing so hard he didn't notice Matt and Chris and Rizzo until they'd braked their bikes right at the curb.

Uh-oh, Jason thought, looking at Matt. He felt a flicker of fear.

"Wheelbarrows?" Chris asked in a high, fake voice. "Oooh, goody!"

"Can I have a ride?" Rizzo begged. "Pretty please?"

"Get lost," Frances said.

Matt just straddled his bike, his arms crossed knowingly across his chest.

Chris and Rizzo aimed their bikes at Flea, made vrooming sounds, and rode straight at him, braking just as they were about to run over his sneakers. Flea flinched and covered his eyes.

"We were just getting wood," Jason said to Matt.

But Matt smiled an evil smile and shook his head. Then he made himself look dopey.

"If you give me a ride in your wheelbarrow," he said, batting his eyes at Jason, "I'll be your best friend forever."

Chris and Rizzo hooted.

"Shut up," Jason said. But he couldn't help adding, "It's for my science project. I'm not hanging around with them or anything."

"I thought you didn't have to do a science project," Matt said.

"Get lost," Frances said again, only this time Jason could feel her looking right at him.

Matt and Chris and Rizzo rode around in the intersection, hollering and laughing, as Jason and the others crossed the street. Then they got bored and rode away.

Jason trudged along behind until Frances turned on him. "You heard me," she said. "I'll get the wood myself. These guys'll help."

"It's my project too," Jason said. He stood his ground. He wasn't going to let some girl tell him what to do. No matter how fast she was.

Everett looked at Jason. His eyes were watery, but his voice was strong. "Just because I have to be nice to you," he said, and then stopped. "Who cares if you come or not?" he finally said.

Jason's face felt hot. Not sweaty hot, but as if he had been stung, or slapped. He followed the others at a distance, unable to hear them over the clatter of their wheelbarrows.

At the fence, gathering wood, he pretended not to notice that no one looked at him or said anything to him. Back at Frances's house, when he said, "I guess I'll be going," no one said a word. Everett looked away.

On the way home, he remembered the time in second grade when Grant glued Dexter McGinnis's pants to his seat. While Dexter was still wearing them. Dexter's mom had had to bring another pair of pants to school. At recess, Ms. Butler had closed the classroom door and pulled him out of his pants.

Jason remembered thinking he'd rather be dead than have a teacher see him in his underwear. Or have other kids wonder whose pants they could glue to a chair, and think of him. He remembered snickering after recess, as the class filed in and Dexter sat all red and sniffly at his seat.

Now he wished he hadn't laughed.

Chapter 12

Saturday, when he woke up, Jason lay in bed and stared at the ceiling.

Six whole days, he thought.

He remembered his old room the way he remembered Sequoia National Park from summer vacation two years ago.

Someplace hard to picture. Someplace he hadn't stayed long.

The trees at the park had been as tall as skyscrapers. Jason had walked around one of them. It was like walking around a house. He had leaned against it and tried to reach around it. Too big. A sign had said the tree was more than seven hundred years old. Jason had closed his eyes. The bark had felt rough under his palms. It had felt as though the tree were a person, an old person who didn't move much anymore, who never went very far away.

Jason's father had stood behind the tree, looking off into the forest. "I wonder if the ranger lives at the ranger station or just works there," he had said, but Jason had pretended not to hear, because he had known that as soon as they got back from vacation, his dad was flying to Santa Fe to sell nails.

He heard the phone ring, and footsteps downstairs, and Aunt Marjorie yelling, "Jason, it's for you!"

His mom was back from the beach.

"When are you coming?" he asked. "When can I go home?"

"Now, sweetie," his mom said, and Jason felt his heart harden.

"You said not long," he said.

"I said not forever," she said, trying to sound cheerful.

"You said" was all he could think to answer.

"Now, Jason," she said. She sighed, and was quiet for a minute. "I've only just found an apartment."

"You did?" Jason brightened. "What's my room like?"

"It's not a room, exactly," Mom said, and paused. "It's a couch."

"A what?"

"There's only one bedroom, sweetie," Mom said. "I'm taking it. For now."

Jason was silent.

"The couch is in the living room. It folds down into a bed. It's very comfortable."

When they went to Aunt Marion's for Christmas, Jason had to sleep on the couch. She didn't even have an extra dresser, so he had to keep his clothes in his suitcase.

"I'm late, Mom," he said. "I have to go."

Then she asked a lot of questions about school and Ms. Baker-Huff and did he have much homework and was he making a lot of friends.

Jason kept thinking about that couch. A couch was a place to take a nap. You weren't supposed to sleep on a couch for the whole night.

When he got off the phone, he looked at the clock. It was ten thirty.

"Ten o'clock," Frances had said last night on the phone. "If you're coming." She'd paused. "I don't care if you do or not."

"I'm coming," Jason had said. He didn't want anyone thinking he was trying to get out of doing his share.

At Frances's house, Mrs. Gormley answered the door. Jason could tell from the way she looked at him that Mrs. Gormley wished Frances knew more girls.

In the backyard, Flea was pulling planks of

lumber from one of the wheelbarrows. Everett and Alvin were pretending to have a sword fight with some of the wood scraps. Frances was studying a book.

"It's my dad's. It shows how to build stuff," she said, holding it up so Jason could see. "It's got a swing in it and everything."

"Cool," Jason said. "But what's everybody doing here?" He leaned closer and whispered, "It's our project."

Frances looked at him. "Helping," she said. "Just for fun."

She turned away.

"Okay," she said in a loud voice. "Now we have to see if we have the right pieces of wood."

Jason looked over Frances's shoulder at the book. "We need four pieces of wood that are one hundred inches long." He closed his eyes and bit his lower lip, thinking. "That's a little over eight feet."

Everyone looked. "There's nothing that long," Flea said.

"Look for four long pieces that are the same length, then," Jason said. "Any length."

They looked some more. At last, Jason spotted two planks that looked about the same.

"How about these?" he asked.

"Lay those over on the grass," Everett said. "Let's see if we can find two more to match."

Everyone rummaged through the piles of wood. It was hard, because the wood was old and splintery.

"Hey! These two!" Alvin cried. Flea and Jason helped him pull two more boards out of the pile and lay them on the lawn.

"They're about the same," Jason said. "One's about a half inch shorter than the others." He shrugged. "It'll just be a tippy swing."

"Let's measure them," Frances said. She pulled a measuring tape out of her back pocket, held the metal tip against one of the planks, and pulled the rest of the tape to the other end. "Eighty-six inches. A little over seven feet," she said.

Jason said, "A tippy and short swing."

Everyone had different jobs to do. Jason got to hammer everything.

It was a warm fall day. Dead leaves skittered across the lawn, blown by a hot wind. The air smelled of smoke and sawdust. Jason hammered nail after nail. At first, some nails went in crooked; once, he smashed his thumb. But after a time, he found his rhythm; he thrilled to hit the nail just so, to feel it sink effortlessly into the wood, the way a perfect free throw whooshed neatly through the hoop.

In the beginning, everyone kind of ignored Jason. He didn't mind, much. It was nice hammering in the sun. It was nice, everyone quietly busy.

"You know, there's a lot of extra wood in here," Alvin said, rummaging around in one of the wheelbarrows.

"Maybe there's enough for a fort," Everett said.

"Hey!" Flea said. "We could camp out in it!"

Jason hammered a nail into a cross rail. He remembered camping out with Grant and DJ.

"We could roast marshmallows," Alvin said.

"And tell ghost stories," Frances said.

"And pee outside," Everett said.

Jason laughed. He loved camping out. He always felt wild, part of the world's wildness, and not afraid of anything. The night air was heavy with the smell of grass and the sound of crickets. Everything tasted good. Even oatmeal.

"If we work on the fort all winter," he said, "we could camp out in the spring."

Everyone was hot and sweaty. They laid down their tools and drank out of the hose and stood around looking at what they'd built so far.

"Like two big A's," Everett said. "Cool."

"I feel just like an ant," Flea said proudly.

Jason and Frances burst out laughing.

"Because ants work together!" he yelled, but they only laughed harder.

For lunch, Mrs. Gormley made them ham

sandwiches. Even though they had big, gloppy slices of tomatoes in them, Jason thought they were the best sandwiches he'd ever eaten.

While they were eating, they told each other the grossest things they could think of because it was funny seeing everyone's reactions. When he couldn't think of anything gross to tell about, Jason thought it was a dumb game, but then he remembered about blindfolding kids and telling them the oatmeal was throw-up. Frances barely rolled her eyes, but Alvin clutched his throat and made gagging noises. Then Everett told about sneezing milk out of his nose, and before he could stop himself, Jason groaned and said, "Sick!"

Everett smiled proudly, as if he'd scored a point in a really tight game.

Out in the backyard after lunch, Frances looked everywhere for her level. "I had it before," she said, looking under pieces of lumber strewn around the yard.

"I see it," Everett said, and he ran to where it lay on the lawn. But running past Jason, he didn't see a stray two-by-four.

Jason reacted before he could think. He reached out and grabbed Everett's arm. He felt him stumble and wobble, but he held on, and Everett didn't fall.

Everett looked at him. "Thanks," he said.

Jason let go of his sleeve. "You're welcome," he said.

Everyone went back to work. But for several minutes, Jason could feel his heart thudding in his chest.

As if he had been running very fast. As if he had just slid into home.

■

They worked all afternoon. It was almost dark by the time they finished.

They stood around the swing, admiring it. Jason wiped his arm across his forehead. His sleeve came away damp.

"I never knew hammering could be such good exercise," he said.

"It's a good thing you found that rope," Everett said. "Otherwise, how would we have hung the swing from the crossbar?"

"My dad only uses it to tie things into his truck," Frances said. "I don't think he'll even know it's gone."

Everyone stood around sweating and feeling proud until Mrs. Gormley came out and reminded Frances that she had to take a bath before they took her grandpa out for Chinese food. Frances made a face, but she got up and went inside.

Jason and Everett walked home in friendly

silence. Jason found a stick to run along a fence. It made a pleasant *thwick*ing sound. Everett kicked a stone along the sidewalk.

"Too bad that wasn't a ball," Jason said as the stone came to rest halfway down the block. "That kick would have gotten you to first base."

Everett found another stone. He maneuvered himself until he was directly behind it, then gave it a solid kick. "If it was a ball," he said, "I wouldn't have even wanted to kick it." He jammed his hands in his pockets. "In case anyone laughed."

"Yeah," Jason said. He watched the stone as it skittered down the sidewalk.

He tried to imagine being a kid and not wanting to kick a ball. He tried as hard as he could. But finally he just gave up.

Chapter 13

"How are the projects coming?" Ms. Baker-Huff asked on Monday.

There were some problems. Jeffrey Martin and Nate Thayer were having trouble cross-pollinating their pea flowers. Chris Doniger and Brian Romero couldn't get their pendulum to swing the right way. Genevieve Bruce still didn't want to touch any ants.

"Ants can't hurt you, Genevieve," Ms. Baker-Huff said.

"They feel creepy on your skin," Genevieve said.

"Aren't you the one who ate snails?" Ms. Baker-Huff asked. "There are worse things to touch than ants, Genevieve."

Flea looked smug.

"Remember, class. Your projects are due on

Friday," Ms. Baker-Huff said. "Please don't forget. No excuses. No unpleasant surprises." She glowered. "Teachers like knowing what to expect."

Who doesn't? thought Jason.

Everett and Frances followed him out to the playground at recess.

"Are you coming over after school?" Frances asked. "We have to put the varnish on."

"Okay," Jason said, "but I can't stay long. I've got something to do tonight."

"I guess we could wait a day," Frances said. "But not any longer. The finish has to dry before Friday."

"Hey, Gallagher!"

Jason looked up to see Matt and some of the guys dribbling a kickball out to the field.

"You coming?"

"In a minute," Jason said.

Matt said something Jason couldn't hear. All the guys laughed. Then he yelled, "Hey, Stinkball! Wanna play kickball?"

"Naw," Everett yelled back, as if Matt were really asking him to play. The guys all laughed some more.

"Jeez, Everett," Jason said. He felt squirmy. "How come you let him call you that?"

"I don't know," Everett said. "I got in the habit."

Jason watched as Matt divided everyone into teams. "Sometimes you should do the opposite of what everyone expects," he said.

Like when I told Matt I wasn't hanging around with Everett and those guys, Jason thought. I should have told him to get lost.

"Hey!" Everett said. "Anybody want to build a sand city?" He took off without waiting for answers, loping toward the sandbox.

Jason looked back out to the field. Matt was ordering everyone around.

Building a sand city turned out to be a lot cooler than Jason had expected. They made roads and tunnels and buildings with doorways.

A bunch of kids Jason had never seen before came over to help. Only one of them was a crummy second grader who tried to wreck everything, and he went away when Jason told him he knew karate.

Once, Jason looked toward the field. Matt was trying to steal third. Jason could tell from how he was leaning, from the way he clenched and unclenched his fists. When at last Matt ran, Jason could almost taste the sweat on his upper lip, could almost smell the dust as it rose behind him.

■

After school, Jason hurried home. He wasn't even going to stop for a snack, but the kitchen smelled like the cinnamon bread Aunt Marjorie had just pulled from the oven.

"Take a break," she said. "Keep me company for a minute."

Jason bit into the bread. It dissolved in a warm, sugary mess in his mouth.

"My mom never makes bread," he said.

"Maybe not," Aunt Marjorie said, drying a dish with a towel. "But she does other things. Did you know your mother won a blue ribbon for canoeing at summer camp?"

Jason didn't think there were many jobs for people who knew how to canoe.

"Aunt Marjorie," he asked, "what did you teach?"

"P.E.," Aunt Marjorie said.

"You're kidding." Jason's jaw dropped. If there'd been any cinnamon bread in his mouth, it would have fallen right out. "Really?"

"Really." Aunt Marjorie hung up the towel. "Why are you so surprised?"

"Because Everett . . ." Jason started to say. "Because he hates sports."

"He doesn't hate them exactly," she said. "He just isn't very good at them."

Jason was stunned. He chewed his bread in silence, and as he chewed, a question began to form in his head.

"But Aunt Marjorie." He stopped. But he had to ask. "What's it like? I mean, Everett being the way he is and . . . I mean . . ."

He didn't know how to ask what he meant. He knew Aunt Marjorie would say stuff about loving Everett no matter what.

"But sometimes," he said, "don't you wish you had a different kind of boy?"

It sounded terrible once he'd said it. He was afraid Aunt Marjorie would be mad.

But she wasn't.

"Have you ever seen a 1969 First Man on the Moon, Jason?"

"What?"

"It's a stamp. And Everett has one that's perfect. Except that when it was printed, someone forgot to use the red ink."

Jason nodded, not understanding.

"There were only about two hundred and fifty First Man on the Moon stamps made without any red ink," Aunt Marjorie said. "And Everett has one of them. It's worth about three hundred dollars," she said proudly.

"Wow."

Aunt Marjorie looked over her shoulder, as though she were checking to make sure no one else could hear. Then she leaned close to Jason's ear.

"Maybe I wish I had someone to play catch with once in a while," she whispered. "Maybe just once in a while." She stood up. "But you should see that First Man on the Moon," she said, shaking her head. "It's really something."

Jason stood up. "I'll play catch with you some-times," he said. "If you want."

Aunt Marjorie smiled. "I'd like that," she said.

He worked upstairs until dinnertime. When Uncle Stewart called him down for dinner, he was almost finished.

"Good for you!" Uncle Stewart said when Jason told him about the swing.

"It sounds like a very interesting project," said Aunt Marjorie, passing rolls.

"It's a very interesting principle," said Uncle Stewart. "It explains how jet planes move, and how rockets are launched. Of course, Isaac Newton didn't build a jet engine, but his principle was a first step." He smeared butter on a roll. "Nothing happens without a first step."

Jason finished working after dinner. While Everett was in the bathroom, he read what he'd written:

Fun Things to Do
with Everett

Talk at night in the dark.
Watch scary movies about aliens and eat popcorn at the same time.
Race wheelbarrows.
Build swings.

Fun Things to Do
with Matt

Play kickball.
Stick things up our noses.

Bad Things about Everett	Bad Things about Matt
Talks all the time.	Is a creep.
Collects stamps which is boring. (Maybe.)	Makes you be a creep when you aren't sure you want to be one.
Can't play sports.	
Everybody thinks he's a loser.	

He made two columns, but he knew what they'd look like even before he'd filled them in.

Total of Fun Things
6

Fun Things to Do with Everett	Fun Things to Do with Matt
$\frac{4}{6} = \frac{2}{3} = 66.67\%$	$\frac{2}{6} = \frac{1}{3} = 33.33\%$

Total of Bad Things
6

Bad Things about Everett	Bad Things about Matt
$\frac{4}{6} = \frac{2}{3} = 66.67\%$	$\frac{2}{6} = \frac{1}{3} = 33.33\%$

He felt like a good scientist. All I have to do now, he thought, is make the right decision.

Chapter 14

The next morning, Jason realized that making the right decision was a lot harder than it seemed.

Just looking at what he'd written, it looked like Everett was more fun than Matt. There were twice as many fun things to do with Everett.

But none of them was as much fun as playing kickball, which was Jason's favorite thing in the world to do.

Jason didn't know how to put that in a column.

"What's your favorite thing in the world to do?" he asked Everett as they walked to school.

"Collect things," Everett said. "Stamps. Bottle caps. Rocks."

"You've sure got a lot of stuff around," Jason said.

"When I was little, I didn't have collections," Everett said. "Then, my favorite thing was repeating everything everybody said."

Jason laughed. "Everything?"

Everett nodded. "Once I repeated everything my mom said for a whole day. 'Good morning, Everett,' she'd say. 'Good morning, Everett,' I'd say. 'Stop it,' she'd say. 'Stop it,' I'd say. It really got on her nerves," he said. "Mom yelled so much I could see the veins in her neck bulging."

"It's hard to picture Aunt Marjorie with bulging veins," Jason said.

"I never knew what to say to people," Everett said. "I thought if I said what everyone else said, no one would notice. Also, it was funny, seeing people react."

He picked up a twig and dropped it down a storm drain. He sighed.

"I called Hilary last night. I told her we can't do anything with a real snake," he said. "I don't know anybody who has one. And besides, you have to feed a snake things like mice that aren't dead yet."

"What'd she say?"

"That only losers are afraid of mice," Everett said. "I'm *not* afraid. I feel sorry for the mice, is all."

"Aren't you sick of everyone calling you a loser all the time?" Jason asked.

"Yes."

They started walking again.

"So what are you going to do?" Jason said to fill up the emptiness where Everett's talking should have been.

"Maybe something with earthworms," Everett said. "Earthworms are as close as I can get to snakes."

Jason played kickball at all three recesses, but he couldn't seem to concentrate. The ball kept slipping out of his hands. Or the sun was always in his eyes. Or he tried to concentrate on the game, but his brain was full of the wrong pictures, of thoughts that should have belonged to some other kid.

"What's the matter with you?" Matt called from the pitcher's mound after Jason missed an easy pop fly.

"You better not screw up," Chris hissed from center field.

"I know," Jason said miserably. But before the bell rang, he had messed up a double play and fouled out twice.

After school Jason went over to Frances's house to varnish the swing. Frances pried open an old can of varnish left over from when her father had built the patio.

"Phew!" she said. "This stuff stinks!"

"I like it," Flea said. "It smells like barbecues and summer."

"Remember the beach?" Everett asked. "Remember the clambake? My favorite thing about summer," he said, "is clambakes."

"What I like best," Alvin said, "is lying in bed on Monday mornings and hearing my grandpa getting ready for work. And knowing I don't have to go anywhere or do anything."

"I like playing baseball with my dad after work," Frances said. "Late. Before the sun goes down. Instead of waiting for weekends." She brushed on some varnish and eyed it critically. "There's more time in the summer," she said.

When nobody was looking, Jason leaned down close to the swing. He closed his eyes and sniffed the wood. The smell of varnish made his eyes water.

He wondered what clams tasted like.

■

As he walked in the kitchen door, he heard Aunt Marjorie say, "There's a letter for you, Jason."

He could see it lying on the front table. He could see the handwriting and the funny stamps. He felt dizzy, the way you felt looking down a sewer grate and not being sure you could stop yourself from jumping in.

He read "Dear Monster Man," and then he

had to stop and close his eyes and take a deep breath.

He read about how neat Australia was, about how there were kangaroos all over the place and how the kids played cricket and rugby instead of baseball. It was pretty in Australia, his father said. Not many trees, but pretty just the same.

Jason felt his heart thudding in his chest. He read:

> It looks like I'll be hanging out here selling
> shingles for a while. A shingle is a part of
> a roof. It's a good thing to be selling.
> Everybody needs to live somewhere. Guess
> I'll be living in Australia unless they send
> me someplace else.

Jason ran down the hall to the bathroom. He flushed the toilet and watched the water gurgle around and down. He flushed the toilet again and again, and remembered Grant and DJ and the mousehole in the wall of his closet where he'd hidden all the bubble gum and mowing the grass on Saturday mornings and the way the rain had sounded late at night and how the basement smelled. And other stuff. And soon it was as if everything he could remember was disappearing, carried away in the swirling, churning water.

The rushing water thundered in his ears, until he realized that the sound of his own sobs was louder.

■

After dinner Jason watched as Everett checked on his earthworms.

"The sand was on top of the soil when I put them in the jar," Everett explained. "Now some of the soil is on top of the sand. That's because the earthworms have been making burrows. They mix up the soil and let air get into it. They make the dirt good for plants and trees."

"Cool," Jason said. "What does Hilary say?"

"That worms aren't as cool as snakes," he said. "And that I have to do all the work because it's my fault we got stuck doing worms."

"I think if Matt Morrison was a girl, he'd be Hilary," Jason said.

Everett laughed. "I don't care," he said almost cheerfully. "I'm glad I know about worms now." He peered into the jar. "I may start a collection."

He got up to go to the bathroom.

When he came back, Jason was wrapping black construction paper around the outside of the jar.

"So the worms will think they're underground," he explained.

"Gee, thanks," Everett said. He looked at Jason. "I just helped you build the swing for fun, you know."

"I know," Jason said.

Chapter 15

Friday morning finally dawned, clear and cool. Everett and Jason ran to Frances's house. Mr. Gormley had already loaded the swing into the back of his pickup truck. The air smelled sharply of varnish.

"Whatever happened to experiments with batteries and magnets?" asked Mr. Gormley. But he looked proud.

There wasn't enough room for everybody in the cab, so Everett and Jason rode in the back, with the swing. Mr. Gormley drove very slowly and took the back roads to school. Still, it seemed dangerous to be riding without seat belts, to have to yell to be heard over the sounds of wind and traffic.

"Hey!" Everett yelled as they thudded over a speed bump. "This is fun!"

"Funner than eating three candy bars and two bags of popcorn at the movies!" Jason yelled back.

Actually, he had done that once. It wasn't so much fun. He'd thrown up six times.

"Funner than camping out in the backyard and eating marshmallows!" Everett yelled.

"Funner than winning a race!" It wasn't, but Jason said it anyway.

They both laughed, because kids in cars were pointing at them and they felt important.

"Funner than beating the sixth graders at kickball," Jason yelled.

"Yeah," Everett said, but he didn't laugh as hard as before.

Jason waited for Everett to think of something else that wasn't as much fun as riding in the truck. But Everett didn't say anything else. They rode the rest of the way to school without talking.

"What have we here?" Ms. Baker-Huff boomed after everyone had sat down. All the kids went "Oooh."

"It's a swing," Jason said proudly, "that we made ourselves."

"With help," Frances added.

"Help from kids," Jason said. He didn't want Ms. Baker-Huff thinking grown-ups had done any of it.

Rosemary raised her hand. "Can we try it?" she asked.

"It's not a toy," Frances said, scowling.

"It's to show action and reaction," Jason said.

"Which is how rockets move," Frances said.

Everyone said "Oooh" again.

"Isaac Newton thought of it," Jason said. He realized he had to talk fast or Frances would say everything. Girls always wanted to say everything while you just stood there.

"He said that for every action there is an equal and opposite reaction," Frances said.

"*Equal* means each reaction is just as strong as the original action," Jason said. He couldn't explain *opposite*. He could only think of examples. Up and down. Straight and crooked. Strong and weak. Kind and mean.

While Frances was telling the class about burning gas molecules, Jason decided it was fun explaining things with Frances. You had to be fast or she'd say stuff first. But if you forgot to tell about how standing on the Earth was like being connected to it, she'd remember.

"So if you're standing on the ground, it looks like nothing happens when you throw the ball," Frances was saying.

"We made a swing so that everyone could see the reaction," Jason said. "Without the swing, you wouldn't be able to see what happens after you throw the ball."

Frances sat in the swing. Jason gave her the ball. She folded up her legs so her feet were off the floor.

The swing creaked. For a second, Jason panicked. What if a nail didn't hold? What if the whole thing fell apart, right there, with Ms. Baker-Huff and all the kids watching?

Frances winced when the swing creaked. But she held her legs up. The freckles on her nose looked shiny. Jason could tell she was gritting her teeth.

"Action and reaction is a scientific principle," Jason told the class. "So it has to be true. Isaac Newton said so."

He steadied the ropes until Frances was perfectly still. "Not too hard," he whispered. He put on his mitt, thumped it with his fist, and backed up.

Frances smiled and threw. Just hard enough. She swung lightly back, then forward, then back again.

"Cool," someone whispered.

Ms. Baker-Huff smiled.

■

At recess, Jason headed out to the field. He could see the sixth grade warming up. They looked big.

"Hey!"

Jason turned around. Everett and Frances, Flea, and Alvin were running behind him, trying to catch up.

"Wait up!" Frances yelled.

"What are you doing out here?" he asked when they reached him.

"We want to watch you get clobbered by the sixth grade," Frances said. But she smiled as she said it.

"Gee, thanks," Jason said.

Matt and the guys ran up behind them.

"The whole school's coming out to watch," Matt said. He sounded serious. "We'd better be good. We'd better win. No way am I losing in front of the whole school."

"Can I play?" Everett asked.

Jason stared.

"What?" Matt asked.

"I said, 'Can I play?'"

Matt hooted. "You?" The guys started to laugh. "Excuse me, Stinkball. This isn't Parcheesi. We're going to play kickball."

Everett didn't say anything. Everyone was looking at him as if he'd just sprouted a second head.

Finally everyone stopped laughing. Matt looked at Everett.

"Well?" Everett said.

Matt got as close to Everett as he could without stepping on his feet. "The last thing I need right now," he said, "is having to teach a loser how to play kickball."

"Morrison," Jason said. Everyone turned to look at him. "I say he plays."

"What?" Matt squeaked. "What's the matter with you?"

"Either he plays," Jason said, "or I don't."

Matt's mouth opened, but no sound came out.

"Hey! Fifth grade!" a big sixth grader yelled. "Let's go!"

Some of the other sixth graders were yelling things like "We don't have all day" and "Chicken!"

Matt looked at Jason. "Aw, come on, Gallagher!" he said. "I told my dad!" His eyes squinted in desperation. His upper lip looked sweaty. "And my dad said no way could fifth-grade weaklings beat the sixth grade."

"You heard me," Jason said calmly.

"Oh, man!" Matt exploded. "All right, all right!" He turned back to Everett. "You better not blow it, you little creep." He put his face nose to nose with Everett's. "You just better not."

He and the guys ran out to warm up.

"Jeez, Everett!" Jason said. "What did you go and do that for?" He combed his hair with his fingers. "Have you ever even played kickball?"

"You said do something no one would expect," Everett said.

"Well, yeah, but I didn't mean now!"

Everett looked at him. "Promise you won't laugh," he whispered.

Jason sighed. "I won't laugh," he said.

Everett stared at the field, where the sixth graders were taking their positions.

"Which one's left field again?" he asked.

Chapter 16

Matt was up first. McCarthy, the biggest sixth grader, was pitching.

On his first pitch, Matt kicked a foul ball.

"Way to go," yelled one of the outfielders. Some of the sixth graders laughed.

"It's weird seeing people making fun of Matt," Jason whispered to Everett. From the dugout, he could see the sweat on the back of Matt's neck.

With the second pitch, Matt made contact. It wasn't much of a kick, but it got him to first base.

The fifth graders cheered, except for Everett, who clapped politely.

Chris Doniger was up next. On his second pitch he kicked a puny pop fly, easily caught by McCarthy.

Jason stood up. "You're up next after me," he whispered to Everett. "Just watch the ball, kick it, and run as fast as you can." He thought a minute. "Pretend it's a stone on the sidewalk." It wasn't much help, but it was all he could think to offer.

Everett nodded seriously.

Jason walked out to the plate. McCarthy was staring at him. He stared back. He stopped thinking about Everett stewing on the bench. Suddenly there was just McCarthy and the ball.

He caught the ball with the top of his shoe, rather than with the toe, as he'd meant to. The ball shot back, higher and slower than Jason would have liked, bounced once, then sailed into the waiting hands of the third baseman.

Jason made it to first with no time to spare. He looked ahead. Matt had made it to second.

With dread, Jason turned to see Everett standing at home plate. He looked small and defenseless, like a raccoon about to be hit by a bus.

"Easy out, easy out," chanted the shortstop.

McCarthy pitched the ball. From first base, Jason could hear its rubbery thump as it rolled out of McCarthy's hands and hit the grass. It thudded down the field, straight at Everett.

Jason saw Everett close his eyes.

Three pitches later, Everett was out. He

shoved his hands deep in his pockets and slunk back to the dugout. Some of the fifth-grade boys booed.

"Thanks, Gallagher," Matt called to Jason from second base. "I'm stranded at second, thanks to you and Stinkball."

But by the end of the first half of the inning, Matt and Jason had scored.

"Look," Matt said to Jason as the fifth grade headed for the field, "I want Stinkball as far out in the outfield as he can get. I don't want him doing any more damage than he's already done."

"He isn't doing any damage," Jason said. "Everybody misses a ball now and then. Like you when Frances Gormley—"

Matt grabbed him by the front of his shirt. "I should have smelled a loser the day I met you," he hissed. "You think it matters how good you are at kickball? Well, it doesn't." He pushed Jason away. "You've got loser in your blood." He stalked out to the pitcher's mound, wiping his hand on his pants leg.

Everett came up behind Jason.

"Where should I go?" he asked. "What do I do now?"

"Go out there. Way out. Just stand there," Jason said. "If the ball rolls to you, pick it up and throw it to Matt. Go way, way out."

The sixth grade was very good at kickball.

Matt tried to psych them out, but by the end of the inning, McCarthy and a guy named Hunsaker had rounded the bases and tied the score.

From his vantage point at second base, Jason got a good look at the bleachers. The game had attracted a lot of attention. Lots of fifth and sixth graders were watching and yelling things at the players. One of the yard-duty monitors stood at the edge of the field, trying to pay attention to the game while she kept her eye on the first-grade sandbox.

Jason searched the stands. He spotted Alvin eating cheese crunchies and licking his fingers. Flea was making faces at Everett. Frances was scowling.

The fifth grade played good defense. The ball never got near Everett.

Back in the dugout, Everett whispered to Jason, "It's boring in the outfield. There's nothing to do out there."

"There is if you ever get the ball," Jason said.

"It's hot out there," Everett whined. "There's no one to talk to."

"For crying out loud," Jason snapped. "You're supposed to be playing kickball. There's not supposed to be any talking."

Everett kicked at some dirt. "It's boring," he said.

How could anyone think kickball was boring?

"You have to think. You have to figure stuff out. Like what will happen if the ball goes deep into right field? Or what if it's fielded by the short-stop? Which base should you throw to? Who's running where? It's so complicated," Jason said. "You have to be ready. You have to know. You can't be surprised. Ever."

Jason was up. Chris was on first. Matt had made it to second.

"Good luck," Everett said.

On the second pitch, Jason kicked a solid grounder into left field. Hunsaker, at third, dove for it and missed. Jason made first easily. Chris stood panting at second. Miraculously, Matt slid untagged into third.

Just great, Jason thought. Bases loaded. Just great.

Everett stood at the plate. He picked wax out of his ear and squinted into the sun.

"Quit stalling, you weenie," yelled the second baseman.

The ball rolled off McCarthy's hand. It thumped and skidded across the grass, and finally collided full force with the toe of Everett's shoe.

It wasn't much of a kick. The ball seemed to stop on contact, then bobbled and weaved uncertainly toward a destination somewhere infield.

Everett looked on in amazement.

"Run!" shouted the fifth graders in the bleachers. Everett looked up at them, then trotted out to first.

McCarthy and the shortstop lunged for the ball, but the shortstop was quicker and closer to the ground. He fielded the ball neatly; machine-like, he threw it to the catcher.

At the sight of the catcher, ball in hand, foot atop home plate, Matt slowed and slapped his thigh.

"Force out!" yelled the sixth graders in the stands.

Matt loped over to the dugout, his face red and damp. Jason, panting for breath at second, saw him slam his fist down on the bench.

"Hey, Jason!" Everett yelled from first. When Jason looked, he waved.

Rizzo was up. His kick sent the ball firmly into right field. Jason tore around the bases. He and Chris made it home.

As his foot touched home plate, Jason turned and looked toward third.

Everett was running for home.

Running fast. As fast as Jason had ever seen anybody run.

"Come on!" Jason screamed. "Run, Everett! Run!"

Everett reached home plate just as the bell rang. Recess was over.

"Fifth grade forever! Fifth grade forever!" chanted the fifth graders in the bleachers.

"No fair!" yelled McCarthy. "You got more ups!"

"You said sudden death! You said!" Chris Doniger yelled back. "Boy, am I hot! Boy, would I like some cool, refreshing frozen yogurt!" He laughed, then ducked as McCarthy threw the kickball at him.

Jason laughed and slapped Everett on the back.

"You scored! Nice going!"

"Thank you," Everett said formally. He was panting. "But we did get more ups. Maybe they're right. Maybe it wasn't fair."

"This is how it works," Jason said. "Whoever scores the most wins. It's how it always is."

Matt was jogging slowly off the field. He looked over as he passed Jason and Everett. "Stick to Barbies," he called to Everett. "Stick to Barbies and ballet, Stinkball."

"Quit calling me Stinkball!" Everett yelled.

Jason's heart froze in his chest.

"He's just mad because he got forced out on your kick," he whispered to Everett.

Matt's mouth hung open. But he didn't say anything.

Chris Doniger ran up from behind. "Aw, leave him alone," he said to Matt. "He did kick the ball."

Matt's mouth snapped shut. For a second he was speechless.

Then he smiled his slow, mean smile.

"If you call that a kick," he said.

Then he took off with Chris and the others.

Frances, Alvin, and Flea caught up. Alvin popped a cheese crunchie in his mouth. "See?" he said, brushing cheese dust off his front. "If you don't play, he hates you. If you do play, he hates you. Nothing ever changes."

"It was cool, though," Everett said. "Telling him to quit calling me Stinkball."

"Did you see his reaction?" Frances said. "He just stood there, looking stupid. I thought he was going to punch your lights out. But he didn't."

Everett didn't wave his arms around, or laugh, or say a word. He just smiled.

Chapter 17

"Everything's settled," Aunt Marjorie said.
"You're staying with us for a while."

The grown-ups had talked. Jason didn't know
when, or what they'd said.

He'd thrown his dad's letter away, but he hadn't
torn it up, and after a day or two he'd dug
around in the wastebasket and found it. He'd
put it in his suitcase, under his bed, in case he
ever wanted to read it again, which he was sure
he wouldn't. He gave the envelope to Everett,
who was excited because he didn't have any
stamps from Australia. He showed Jason just
where in his album they belonged.

Jason had never seen so many old stamps.
Everett showed him some with pictures of old
war guns and dead presidents on them. He had
never thought much about stamps before. For

the first time, he noticed the colors, the details in the designs.

Jason's mom called him a lot. She had finally gotten a job as a switchboard operator in a hospital. She sent out ambulances and called doctors at home when someone needed to have a baby or an appendix taken out or something. Jason thought it sounded cool, but his mom was always tired. She had to work at night and take her clothes to the Laundromat because her building didn't have a washer and dryer.

"I think it would be fun to work at night and sleep all day," Jason said, but his mom didn't say anything.

When he hung up, he realized that if she worked at night, there wouldn't be anyone around to take care of him.

"I should have known," he said to Everett on the way to Alvin's.

"How?" Everett asked. "How were you supposed to know?"

"I just should have," Jason said. Like when someone pitched you a curve ball. "I should have seen it coming."

He waited for Everett's nervous laughter, but Everett was quiet.

■

Everyone was glad Jason wasn't leaving.

"I didn't even get to show you my ant farm," Flea said.

The others snuck looks at each other, because even when you liked someone, sometimes you got sick of their hobbies.

"I like dogs," Jason said. Two weeks ago he'd probably have said, "Ants are stupid pets." But now he just kept quiet. You never knew. Maybe he'd find out about ants and like them as much as dogs.

Probably not. But you never knew for sure.

He thumped his mitt with his fist and waited for Alvin to throw him the ball.

"Are you sure I'm doing this right?" Alvin said. He threw the ball to Jason, who had to stretch to make the catch. "Dogs make me break out."

Maybe some things you could know for sure, Jason decided, throwing the ball to Everett, and knowing ahead of time that he would miss the catch.

"Don't they teach this stuff in school?" he asked.

"Yeah," Everett said, "but Mr. Perkillo gets tired of showing the kids who don't know how. He lets us jog around the playground instead." He threw the ball to Frances, who leaned forward to field it. Jason watched admiringly as the ball came to rest neatly in her glove.

"Nice one," he said.

Frances flashed him a small smile.

Everett looked at his watch.

"You said half an hour, Jason. Just half an hour. And then we can go in and play with Alvin's trains. You said."

"Jeez, Everett," Jason said. "It's a lot more fun to play catch if you don't wait for it to be over." But after a few more throws, they went inside.

The only things in the refrigerator were rice pudding and cranberry juice.

"Don't you have anything like Popsicles?" Jason asked.

"We don't eat regular food," Alvin said. "My grandpa has never eaten a pizza."

"You're kidding," Jason said.

Alvin shrugged. "He says he'd just as soon have a cheese sandwich."

They sat down at the kitchen table. Alvin dug around in a drawer for spoons.

Suddenly Jason felt sad, as if sadness were a wave that had knocked him down. He didn't want to be eating rice pudding with a bunch of kids who couldn't wait to stop playing ball. Frances liked playing ball and knew about action and reaction, but she was still just a dumb old girl with freckles who had to take ballet.

The rice pudding on his plate looked gray and globby. "This stuff looks disgusting," he said meanly.

"You better not let my grandma hear you," Alvin said. "It's her special recipe."

"Try it," Everett said gently. "It's not so bad."

Jason looked down at his plate. He thought of Grant and DJ and the oatmeal they'd pretended was throw-up. Grant and DJ wouldn't eat disgusting food. They would make other kids sick with it. Or play with it until a grown-up felt sorry for them and took it away. Or feed it to the cat when no one was looking.

He missed Grant and DJ so much that it was like getting socked in the stomach. It was like missing his mom and his dad and his own room and how everyone at his old school had thought he was cool and he hadn't even known it. All at once.

It was awful. He thought he might cry.

To stop himself, he took a bite of rice pudding. He held his breath and scrunched up his eyes, but the pudding was sweet and smooth and good.

"Hey," he said.

"See?" Alvin said triumphantly,

"I told you it was good," Everett said.

Jason took another bite. "Well, not terrible, anyway," he said.

"We know," Flea said. "We eat it here all the time."

"Unless Mrs. Jamison makes prune whip," Frances said. "I love prune whip."

Alvin licked his spoon. "Come on," he said. "Doesn't anyone want to play trains?"

"No," Jason said. But he took his plate to the sink with everyone else.

They clomped down the stairs to the basement. Jason thought it was stupid to spend time in a basement when he could just as well be outside throwing a ball.

"Doesn't anyone want to practice fielding grounders?" he asked.

Frances looked over at him. "Maybe later," she said, smiling.

Jason sighed. He knew he would have to settle for that.

In the murky half-light, Alvin checked to make sure that all the train cars' wheels sat properly on the tracks. He fiddled with wires and plugs. He seemed to want everything to be just so. Like a scientist who wanted his experiment to come out right, Jason thought.

Alvin flicked a switch. The engine's headlight shone. Slowly the train pulled out of the station.

Jason stood behind the others, watching, hearing the clicking and whirring of the cars along the track. He liked the way they went through tunnels and how they looked going around turns. He imagined the passengers: little families hurtling into the unknown around the corner, snug and unafraid in their gently pitch-

ing cars. Knowing that home was out there somewhere; that until they got there they would be
all right. Safe.

"Want to man the controls?" Alvin asked, passing Jason the control box. It was small and
heavy in his hands. He eased the On lever down,
and the train chugged slowly forward.

"Cool," he said.

He had to be careful going around turns.
When he pushed the lever down too hard, the
train took the turn too fast and jumped the
tracks.

"It takes practice," Everett said as Alvin righted
the engine and realigned its wheels.

Jason smiled and nodded. And by the time
Mrs. Jamison called down to say that dinner was
ready, he almost had it.